I LUKE.

I OVE I Love
LeLoLWVeL

OVeLLWeLeL
i. VeLeLeL.

YeLoLeL.
VeVKenne

CHILDREN'S ENCYCLOPEDIA
SPACE

CHILDREN'S ENCYCLOPEDIA
SPACE

Miles Kelly

First published in 2015 by Miles Kelly Publishing Ltd
Harding's Barn, Bardfield End Green, Thaxted, Essex, CM6 3PX, UK

2 4 6 8 10 9 7 5 3 1

Publishing Director Belinda Gallagher
Creative Director Jo Cowan
Editorial Director Rosie Neave
Cover Designer Simon Lee
Designers Jo Cowan, D&A, Rob Hale, Joe Jones,
Andrea Slane
Editors Carly Blake, Fran Bromage, Amy Johnson,
Rosie Neave, Sarah Parkin
Indexers Eleanor Holme, Jane Parker
Image Manager Liberty Newton
Production Elizabeth Collins, Caroline Kelly
Reprographics Stephan Davis, Jennifer Cozens, Thom Allaway
Contributors Sue Becklake, Clive Gifford, Ian Graham,
Steve Parker, Clint Twist

ISBN 978-1-78209-793-8

Printed in China

British Library Cataloguing-in-Publication Data
A catalogue record for this book is available from the British Library

Made with paper from a sustainable forest

www.mileskelly.net
info@mileskelly.net

CONTENTS

SOLAR SYSTEM 8–49

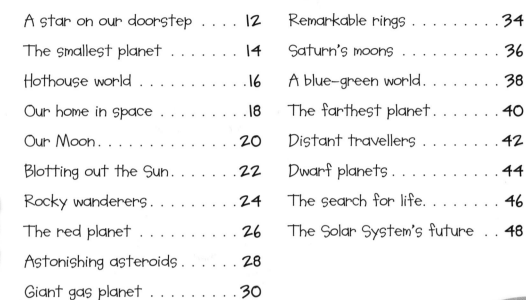

STARS AND GALAXIES 50–91

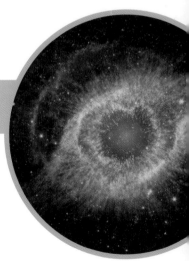

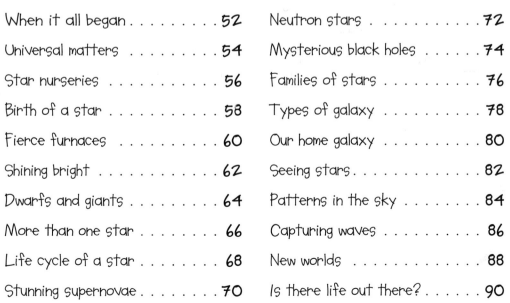

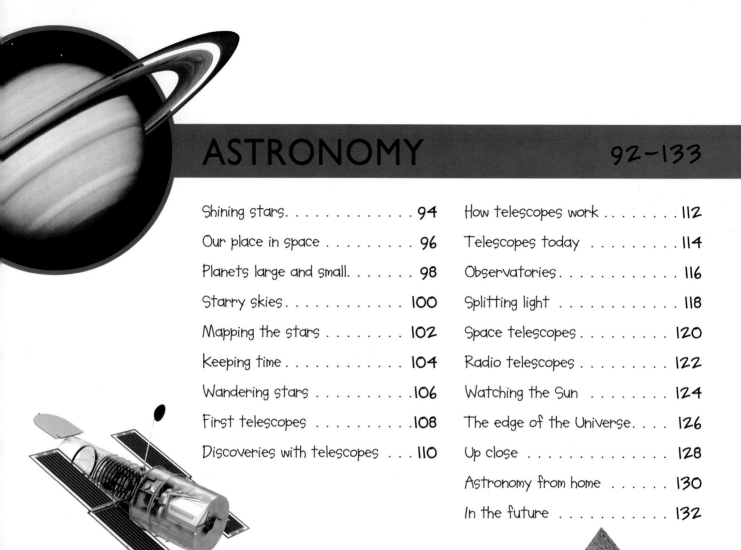

ASTRONOMY 92–133

Shining stars. 94

Our place in space 96

Planets large and small. 98

Starry skies. 100

Mapping the stars 102

Keeping time. 104

Wandering stars 106

First telescopes 108

Discoveries with telescopes . . . 110

How telescopes work 112

Telescopes today 114

Observatories. 116

Splitting light 118

Space telescopes 120

Radio telescopes 122

Watching the Sun 124

The edge of the Universe. . . . 126

Up close 128

Astronomy from home 130

In the future 132

EXPLORING SPACE 134–175

Who explores, and why? 136

Early explorers 138

Man on the Moon! 140

Plan and prepare 142

Blast-off!. 144

In deep space 146

Ready to explore. 148

Flyby, bye-bye. 150

Into orbit 152

Landers and impactors 154

Robotic rovers 156

Close-up look 158

Exploring Mars 160

Back on Earth. 162

Towards the Sun 164

Asteroids near and far. 166

Comet mysteries 168

Gas giants 170

Into the future 172

Space magic and myth 174

SPACE TRAVEL  176–217

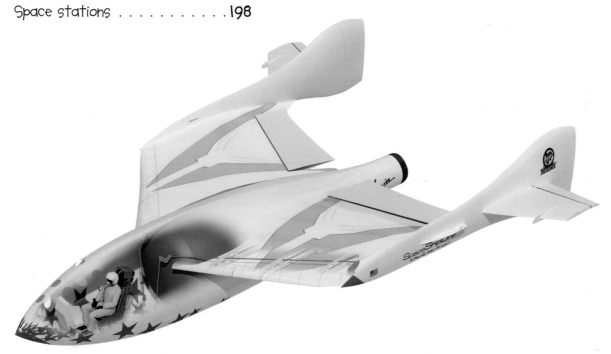

SOLAR SYSTEM

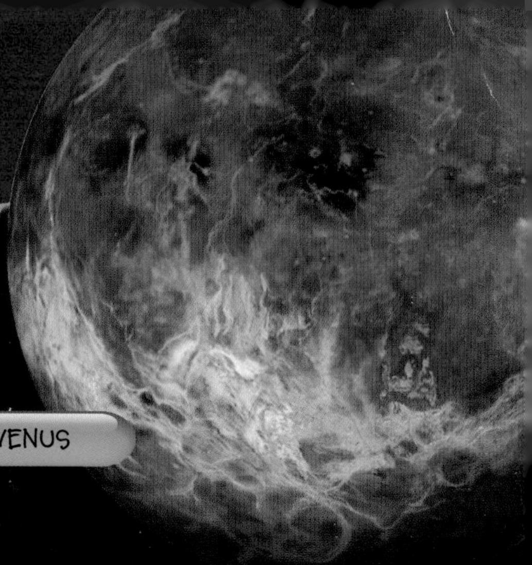

VENUS

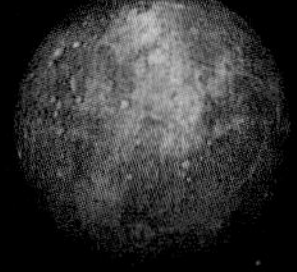

MERCURY

EARTH

1 The Solar System consists of the Sun and everything that orbits (moves around) it. Eight planets orbit the Sun, and more than 160 smaller moons orbit the planets. There are also millions of other objects circling the Sun, including asteroids and comets. The pull of the Sun's gravity holds the Solar System together.

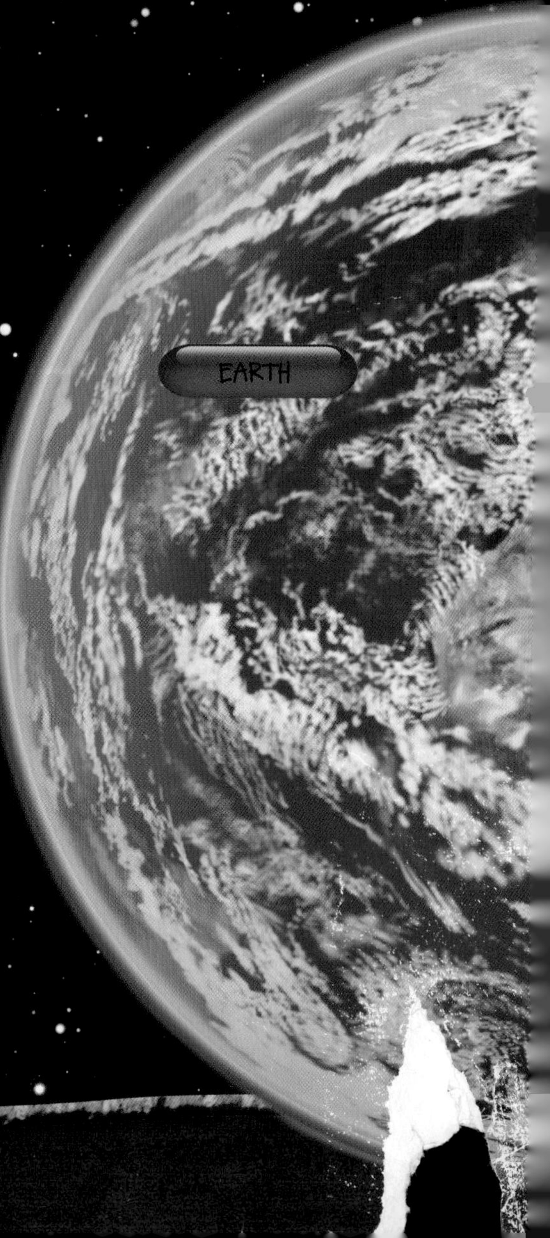

URANUS

SATURN

NEPTUNE

MARS

▼ The four planets closest
to the Sun – Mercury,
Earth, Venus and Mars –
are smaller and made of
rock. The four farthest
from the Sun – Jupiter,
Saturn, Uranus and
Neptune – are bigger and
made of gas and liquid.

JUPITER

Where did it all come from?

2 The Solar System began as a vast, swirling cloud of gas and dust called a nebula. Most of it was made of hydrogen, the lightest and most common element in the Universe.

3 Around 4.6 billion years ago, the Solar System began to form. It may have been started by the huge explosion of a star – a supernova. Shock waves from the giant explosion would have compressed (squashed) the nebula. Gravity then took over, pulling the nebula inwards and causing it to collapse in on itself.

▼ An area of the Orion nebula in which new stars are forming. Billions of years ago, a nebula like this contained everything needed for the Solar System to form.

▼ This photograph of the remains of a star that exploded in 1572 has been coloured to show what's happening inside it.

Gas and particles (green and yellow) are flying out in all directions

The outside edge of the explosion, called a shock wave, is shown in blue

Hot dust (red) was made when the star exploded

QUIZ

1. How old is the Solar System?
2. What is the most common element in the Universe?
3. What is a nebula?

Answers:
1. Around 4.6 billion years
2. Hydrogen 3. A vast cloud of gas and dust

4 As the nebula collapsed inwards, it started spinning. Clumps of gas and dust formed in the collapsing cloud and grew bigger as gravity pulled more and more gas and dust towards them. A dense mass formed at the centre of the nebula, which increased in temperature and eventually became our Sun. The remaining gas and dust flattened into a spinning disc, later forming the planets.

5 There are still signs of the spinning motion of the shrinking nebula today. The Sun, planets and moons all spin, and the planets travel around the Sun.

▼ It took about 100 million years for the planets to form from the nebula.

1. Dust particles and tiny bits of rock in the spinning disc clumped together.

3. The balls of rock and gas grew bigger and bigger, eventually forming the planets.

2. As these clumps grew bigger their gravity pulled more dust and rock towards them.

11

A star on our doorstep

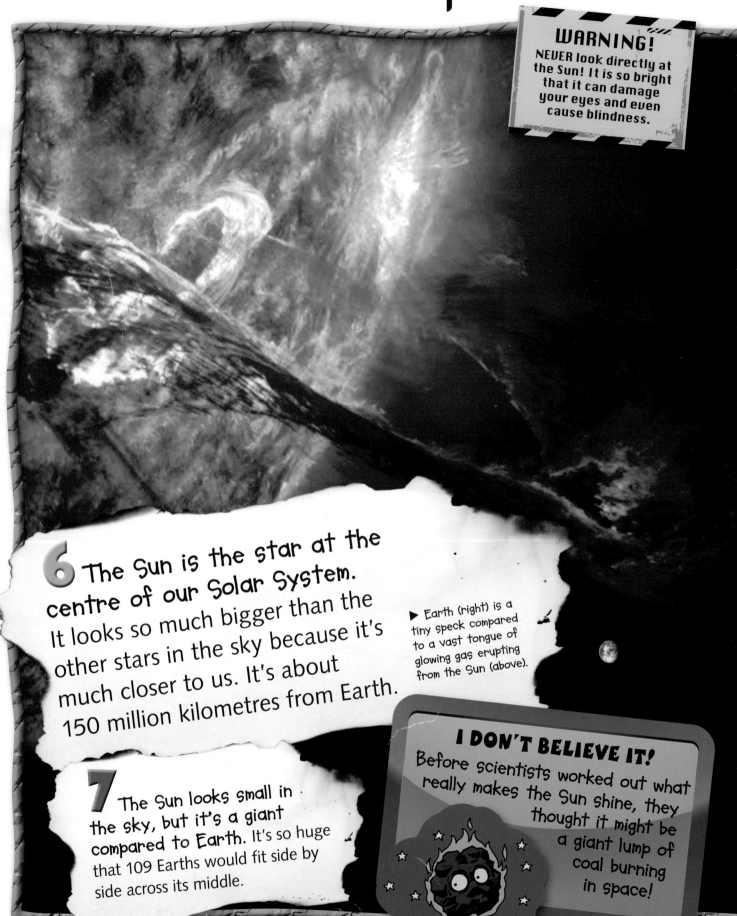

WARNING!
NEVER look directly at the Sun! It is so bright that it can damage your eyes and even cause blindness.

6 The Sun is the star at the centre of our Solar System. It looks so much bigger than the other stars in the sky because it's much closer to us. It's about 150 million kilometres from Earth.

▶ Earth (right) is a tiny speck compared to a vast tongue of glowing gas erupting from the Sun (above).

7 The Sun looks small in the sky, but it's a giant compared to Earth. It's so huge that 109 Earths would fit side by side across its middle.

I DON'T BELIEVE IT!
Before scientists worked out what really makes the Sun shine, they thought it might be a giant lump of coal burning in space!

8 The Sun is made of super-hot gases — mostly hydrogen and helium. Its core (centre) is the hottest part. The temperature here is as high as 15 million°C.

▶ Gravity tries to make the Sun smaller while heat from the core tries to make it bigger. The two are in balance.

10 About four million tonnes of the Sun's mass vanishes every second! This happens because nuclear fusion changes some of the Sun's mass into energy. The Sun has been losing this huge amount of mass every second for about 4.6 billion years.

9 Scientists worked out how the Sun shines in the 1920s. The extremely high pressure in the Sun's core causes particles of hydrogen to smash into each other and fuse (stick together) to form a new substance, helium. This is called nuclear fusion. Every time it happens, energy is given out.

Corona
The outer part of the Sun's atmosphere

Chromosphere
The lowest layer of the Sun's atmosphere

Photosphere
The visible surface of the Sun

Core
Nuclear reactions give out energy

Convective zone
Hot gas rises towards the surface, and falls back inside the Sun in currents

Radiative zone
Energy radiates out from the core

▼ Light and warmth from the Sun sustain life on Earth.

11 Energy produced by nuclear fusion travels from the Sun's core to its surface. This takes up to 200,000 years. Then when it leaves the Sun, it takes just over eight minutes to reach Earth.

The smallest planet

12 Mercury is the Sun's closest planet. It's also the smallest in the Solar System – a tiny planet less than half the size of Earth. It is made of rock with a big iron core, and is very dense for its size.

13 Planets closer to the Sun have to travel through space faster than those farther away, or they would be pulled into the Sun. Mercury's orbit takes 88 Earth days. However, it spins so slowly that a day on Mercury lasts 176 Earth days.

▼ Mercury is a small world that looks similar to Earth's Moon.

14 Mercury has one of the biggest impact craters in the Solar System. It's called the Caloris Basin and it measures 1550 kilometres across. It was caused when an object about 100 kilometres across smashed into Mercury.

The Caloris Basin is a vast shallow crater, surrounded by mountains 2 kilometres high

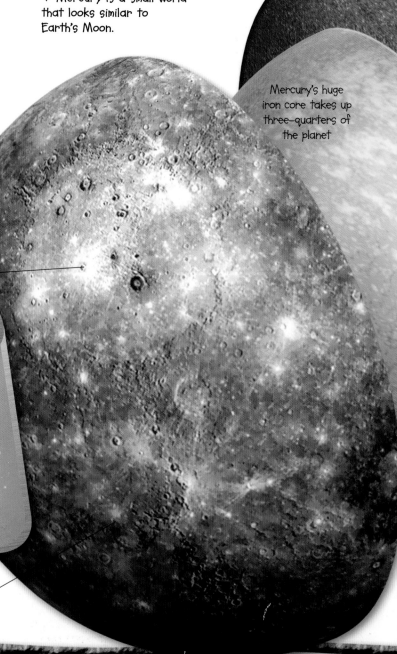

Mercury's huge iron core takes up three-quarters of the planet

Fact file: MERCURY

Named after: The messenger of the Roman gods
Diameter: 4879 kilometres (0.38 times Earth)
Distance from the Sun: 58 million kilometres
Time to spin once: 59 days
Time to orbit the Sun: 88 days
Average temperature: 167°C
Number of moons: 0

The surface of Mercury is scarred by thousands of craters

15 The side of Mercury that faces the Sun reaches up to 430°C. That's hot enough to melt tin! The temperature on the side facing away from the Sun drops to −180°C. That's the biggest difference in temperature between the two sides of any planet in the Solar System.

A thin crust of rock floats on top of the mantle

16 Only two spacecraft have visited Mercury so far. Mariner 10 was the first in the 1970s. A second spacecraft called Messenger arrived in 2008. A third spacecraft, BepiColombo, is due to launch in 2016.

◄ Mariner 10 took the first close-up photographs of Mercury as it flew past in 1974.

A layer of rock, called the mantle, surrounds the core

▲ Messenger was the first spacecraft to go into orbit around Mercury, in 2011.

▲ Engineers prepare the BepiColombo space probe for tests to make sure everything works.

15

Hothouse world

17 **The second planet from the Sun, Venus, is about the same size as Earth.** It is also the closest planet to Earth, although the two are very different. Its rocky surface is hidden under a very thick carbon dioxide atmosphere that traps the Sun's heat, making it the Solar System's hottest planet.

▲ Venus is surrounded by a thick blanket of sulphuric acid clouds.

► Venus is one of the brightest objects in the sky, because its thick clouds reflect a lot of sunlight.

Venus

18 **Venus spins more slowly than other Solar System planets.** It takes 243 Earth days to spin around once, compared to just 24 hours for Earth. Venus spins in the opposite direction to the other planets – the Sun rises in the east on Earth, but in the west on Venus.

I DON'T BELIEVE IT!

Venus's atmosphere is so dense that it has about 90 times the pressure of Earth's. You would need a spacecraft as strong as a submarine to land on Venus.

19 **One way to see Venus's surface is to use radar.** Radar can send radio waves from a spacecraft, through a planet's atmosphere to bounce off the surface below. Analyzing these reflections reveals the shape of the surface.

20

Venus is a very volcanic planet, or at least it was in the past. Its surface is dotted with over 1000 volcanoes – more than any other planet in the Solar System. It is difficult to tell if they are still erupting today.

▶ The surface of Venus is smooth in places, but it also has mountains, volcanoes, craters and canyons.

Fact file: VENUS

Named after: The Roman goddess of love and beauty
Diameter: 12,104 kilometres (0.95 times Earth)
Distance from the Sun: 108 million kilometres
Time to spin once: 243 days
Time to orbit the Sun: 225 days
Average temperature: 464°C
Number of moons: 0

▶ Watching Venus (the big black dot) crossing the Sun gave scientists enough information to work out the size of the Solar System.

21

The famous explorer Captain James Cook sailed from England to Tahiti to see Venus crossing between Earth and the Sun in 1769. The crossing was important to astronomers because they could use it to work out the size of the Solar System. By observing the time it took for Venus' shadow to cross the Sun, astronomers were able to calculate the distance between Earth and Venus.

▶ Captain James Cook and Charles Green, the astronomer on the expedition, both made drawings of Venus crossing the Sun.

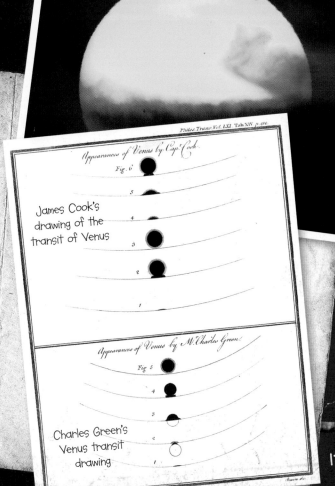

James Cook's drawing of the transit of Venus

Charles Green's Venus transit drawing

Our home in space

22 Earth is the third planet from the Sun. It is the only place in the Universe known to have liquid water and the ability to support life. It takes 24 hours to spin once, giving us night and day, and 365 days (a year) to orbit the Sun.

23 One of the rocky planets, Earth consists of several layers. The thin crust of rock that forms its surface sits on top of a deeper layer of rock called the mantle. Below the mantle, in the middle of the planet, there is a solid iron core with liquid iron around it.

► Life on Earth began in the oceans about 3.8 billion years ago and then spread across the whole planet.

24 Earth's atmosphere is a mixture of gases, mainly nitrogen and oxygen. It also contains some water vapour, carbon dioxide and tiny traces of other gases. This mixture of gases is called air, and without it life on Earth would not be possible.

◄ Earth's core is as hot as the surface of the Sun.

Crust

Upper mantle

Lower mantle

Liquid outer core

Solid inner core

5500°C   5000°C   4000°C   2000°C

I DON'T BELIEVE IT!
A day on Earth is 24 hours long today, but billions of years ago Earth was spinning much faster. A day was only 14 hours long. Earth's spin has been slowing down ever since.

▼ The weather changes from one season to the next because of Earth's tilt.

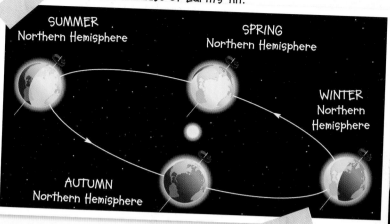

SUMMER
Northern Hemisphere

SPRING
Northern Hemisphere

WINTER
Northern Hemisphere

AUTUMN
Northern Hemisphere

▼ Earth's magnetic field extends far out into space. It protects us from the 'solar wind' – charged particles streaming out of the Sun.

North Pole

South Pole

25 Earth tilts as it travels around the Sun, like a spinning top leaning over. This tilt produces the seasons. When the North Pole tilts towards the Sun, the northern half of Earth is warmer and the southern half is colder. As Earth moves around the Sun, the North Pole tilts away from the Sun. The northern half of Earth cools and the southern half warms up.

26 Earth behaves like a giant magnet with a north pole and a south pole. Liquid iron swirling around in Earth's core creates electrical currents that produce its magnetic field.

27 Particles flying out of the Sun cause an eerie glow in the sky called an aurora. Earth's magnetic field steers the particles into the upper atmosphere near the North and South poles. Here they collide with particles of gas, making them glow.

Fact file: EARTH

Named after: An old English word for the ground or soil
Diameter: 12,756 kilometres
Distance from the Sun: 149.6 million kilometres
Time to spin once: 23.9 hours
Time to orbit the Sun: 365.2 days
Average temperature: 15°C
Number of moons: 1

◀ Auroras light up the sky near the poles, seen from the International Space Station (left). They are known as the Northern Lights (*Aurora Borealis*) and Southern Lights (*Aurora Australis*).

Our Moon

28 Earth has one moon orbiting it. The Moon is made of rock, and is about 384,000 kilometres from Earth. It is just over a quarter of the size of Earth. The Moon's surface is as dry as dust, and covered with thousands of craters made by rocks crashing into it from space.

▶ The big, dark patches on the Moon's surface were once thought to be seas. They are actually volcanic plains formed by lava flows that took place billions of years ago.

29 Scientists think the Moon was part of Earth until about 4.4 billion years ago. Soon after Earth formed, a Mars-sized object crashed into it. The impact knocked chunks of rock out of Earth. The debris collected together, forming the Moon. Life never began on the Moon, as its gravity wasn't strong enough to hold onto an atmosphere.

▼ The Moon exists because of a cosmic collision billions of years ago.

3. The rock clumps together to form the Moon

1. A large wandering body collides with Earth

2. Rock from Earth as well as the destroyed body swirls around Earth

30 From Earth, we always see the same side of the Moon. This happens because the Moon spins at the same speed as it travels around Earth. The Moon's far side was seen for the first time when the Soviet *Luna 3* space probe photographed it in 1959. The first people to see the far side with their own eyes were the crew of the American *Apollo 8* mission in December 1968.

▲ The first image of the far side of the Moon. The far side has a thicker crust, and more craters than the side we see from Earth.

31 The tides that rise and fall on Earth are caused by the Moon. The Moon's gravity pulls Earth's oceans towards it. The water piles up in a big swollen bulge on one side of Earth, with another bulge on the opposite side. As Earth spins, these piles of water sweep around the planet, causing the high tides.

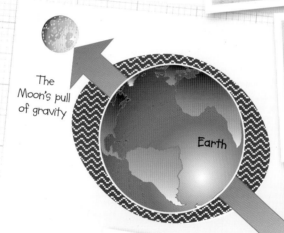

The Moon's pull of gravity

Earth

▶ The Moon's gravity creates two high tides every day.

High tide

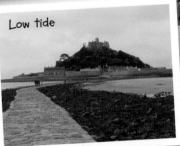

Low tide

▲ When the high tide passes, the sea level falls.

When the Sun, Moon and Earth are aligned, the added pull of the Sun's gravity creates extra-high tides

32 The Moon is much smaller than Earth, so its pull of gravity is weaker. Gravity gives you your weight, so you would weigh less on the Moon than on Earth. The Apollo astronauts who landed on the Moon weighed just one-sixth of their Earth weight while on the Moon.

Blotting out the Sun

33 The Moon sometimes passes between the Sun and Earth, casting a shadow on Earth. This is a solar eclipse. If it looks like the Moon is taking a bite out of the Sun, it's a partial eclipse. If the Moon covers the whole Sun, it's a total eclipse.

34 During a total solar eclipse, the Sun disappears behind the Moon, leaving just its bright corona (atmosphere) visible. It shows up as a glowing ring of light around the Moon. The Sun's atmosphere is incredibly hot – it reaches more than one million°C.

WARNING!
NEVER look directly at the Sun! It is so bright that it can damage your eyes and even cause blindness.

▼ These photographs, taken every four minutes, show a total solar eclipse from start to finish.

▼ The time during which the Moon completely hides the Sun is called totality.

FUTURE TOTAL ECLIPSES

DATE	VISIBLE FROM
9 March, 2016	Sumatra, Borneo, Sulawesi, Pacific Ocean
21 August, 2017	N Pacific Ocean, US, S Atlantic Ocean
2 July, 2019	S Pacific Ocean, Chile, Argentina
14 December, 2020	S Pacific Ocean, Argentina, Chile, S Atlantic Ocean

35

During a total solar eclipse, the Moon's shadow races across Earth at 1700 kilometres an hour. As darkness covers the land, birds and animals fall silent. They think night has come early!

▼ During a total solar eclipse, the Moon blocks light rays from the Sun. People within the inner part of the Moon's shadow see a total eclipse. Those in the outer shadow see a partial eclipse.

Partial solar eclipse
Total solar eclipse
Earth
Moon
Partial solar eclipse
Sun

36

How can the tiny Moon blot out the giant Sun? By a strange quirk of nature, the Moon is not only 400 times smaller than the Sun, it is also 400 times closer to Earth than the Sun. So, from Earth, the Sun and Moon look exactly the same size. This doesn't happen anywhere else in the Solar System.

▼ During a total lunar eclipse, the Moon doesn't disappear completely. Sunlight passing through Earth's atmosphere falls on the Moon and often turns it red.

37

The Sun, Earth and Moon can line up in a different way. If Earth comes between the Sun and Moon, it casts a shadow on the Moon. This is a lunar eclipse. Lunar eclipses can be partial or total. There are at least two lunar eclipses every year.

► A lunar eclipse occurs when the Moon moves through the Earth's shadow.

Sun
Earth
Partial lunar eclipse
Moon
Total lunar eclipse
Partial lunar eclipse

Rocky wanderers

38 If you see a streak of light in the sky, it's probably a meteor, or 'shooting star' (although they are not stars). Meteors are glowing streaks of light caused by pieces of space rock and dust burning up as they enter Earth's atmosphere.

▲ Meteors streak across the sky in this picture of a meteor shower.

39 Smaller space rocks burn up in the atmosphere, but bigger pieces can reach the ground. These cosmic arrivals are called meteorites. Most are small and land unseen, but sometimes a big one lands.

▲ This fireball was caught on camera over Chelyabinsk, Russia, on 15 February, 2013. It was caused by a space rock entering Earth's atmosphere from space and exploding over the city.

► Antarctica is a good place for meteorite-hunting, because the dark meteorites stand out from the white snow.

40 There are three main types of meteorites. They are stony (made of rock), iron (made of metal) and stony-iron (a mixture of rock and metal). Stony meteorites are the most common.

▲ Iron meteorites were once part of the core of a planet, moon or asteroid.

▲ Stony meteorites are made of minerals called silicates.

▲ Stony-iron meteorites contain equal amounts of metal and stone.

41 The biggest meteorite ever found in one piece weighs over 60 tonnes. It is a huge lump of metal known as the Hoba meteorite. It landed in Namibia, in Africa, around 80,000 years ago.

▼ The Hoba meteorite lay buried until a farmer discovered it in 1920 while ploughing his land. It remains in the same spot today.

FIND A METEORITE
You will need:
a magnet

Nearly all meteorites, even the stony ones, contain iron, so they can be picked up by a magnet. Look for dark, smooth, rounded rocks that are attracted to a magnet and feel heavy for their size.

42 Some meteorites come from the Moon or Mars. They were blasted out of the surface by other rocks smashing into them. They roamed the Solar System for millions of years before landing on Earth.

The red planet

43 Mars, the fourth planet from the Sun, is known as 'the red planet' due to its colour. It is the last of the terrestrial (Earth-like) planets, which are all made of rock and thought to have an iron core.

▼ The surface of Mars is a vast desert of fine red sand. It is dry, dusty and extremely cold, and has an atmosphere of poisonous carbon dioxide.

Fact file: MARS

Named after: The Roman god of war
Diameter: 6792 kilometres (0.53 times Earth)
Distance from the Sun: 228 million kilometres
Time to spin once: 24.6 hours
Time to orbit the Sun: 687 days
Average temperature: -65°C
Number of moons: 2

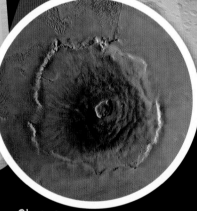

Olympus Mons

Valles Marineris

44 Mars has the biggest volcano in the Solar System, Olympus Mons. It's almost three times higher than Mount Everest. Mars also has one of the biggest canyons, Valles Marineris. It's nine times longer, 20 times wider and more than four times deeper than the Grand Canyon.

I DON'T BELIEVE IT!
In the 1890s astronomer Percival Lowell was convinced he could see canals on Mars, and that they must have been built by Martians. It was later proven that the canals didn't exist.

45 The north and south poles of Mars are covered with ice. They stay frozen all year round. During the Martian winter the poles get so cold that carbon dioxide from the atmosphere freezes onto them.

46 More than 20 spacecraft have been sent to Mars since the 1960s. They have flown past it, orbited it and landed on it. Four rovers have explored its surface. *Sojourner* was tiny, the size of a shoebox. *Spirit* and *Opportunity* were the size of golf buggys. *Curiosity* is the biggest yet, a nuclear-powered rover the size of a small car.

▼ The *Curiosity* rover was sent to Mars to explore its desert-like surface.

26 November, 2011:
The rover is launched onboard an *Atlas 5* rocket. It is heading for a landing site in Gale Crater, 566 million kilometres away.

6 August, 2012:
Curiosity is lowered onto the Martian surface by a rocket-powered Sky Crane. The landing is a success.

29 August, 2012:
Curiosity begins its first drive to an area called Glenelg, about 400 metres from its landing site.

27 September, 2012:
Curiosity returns images of what appears to be an ancient riverbed.

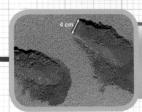
10 October, 2012:
Curiosity collects its first sample of Martian soil. The sample will be analyzed by its onboard instruments.

3 December, 2012:
Through analzying soil, *Curiosity* discovers the first clear evidence that water once existed on Mars.

5 June, 2013:
Curiosity prepares for its trip to the base of Mount Sharp, a journey of about 8 kilometres over rough terrain.

esuit and vehicle sted for a future ion to Mars.

47 There are plans to send astronauts to Mars later this century. A spaceflight would take up to nine months. Astronauts would then have to stay on Mars for another 18 months before the planets are close enough again for the return journey to Earth.

Astonishing asteroids

▼ Hundreds of thousands of asteroids orbit the Sun beyond the four inner planets. They are remains of the Solar System's formation.

48 Asteroids are huge chunks of rock and metal circling the Sun. Most orbit in a band between Mars and Jupiter called the Asteroid Belt. The biggest, Ceres, is 950 kilometres across.

49 Asteroid means 'star-like', because from Earth, asteroids look like tiny points of light. Astronomers can tell the difference between stars and asteroids because asteroids cross the sky faster than stars and often in a different direction. As an as spins, the amount of light i reflects varies. By measuri changes in brightness, astronomers can tell tha asteroids spin every 6–1

50 Some asteroids have their own moons. When the *Galileo* spacecraft was travelling through the Asteroid Belt on its way to Jupiter in 1993, it spotted an asteroid, named Ida, with a tiny moon orbiting it. It was the first asteroid found with its own moon. More than 150 asteroids are now known to have moons.

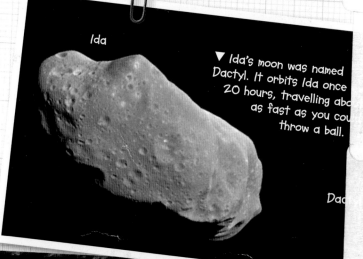

Ida

▼ Ida's moon was named Dactyl. It orbits Ida once 20 hours, travelling abo as fast as you cou throw a ball.

Dac

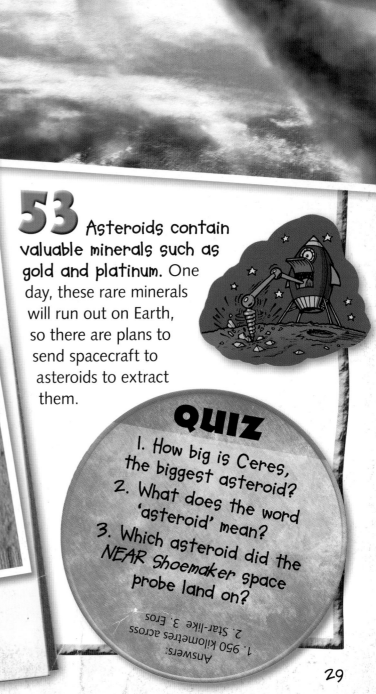

▶ The dinosaurs may have died out 66 million years ago when a large asteroid like this slammed into Earth.

51 Asteroids sometimes wander into our part of the Solar System. Asteroids that come close to Earth are called Near Earth Asteroids (NEAs). Over 10,000 NEAs have been discovered, but only a few hundred of them are big enough to be dangerous to Earth. Space is so vast that asteroids rarely hit Earth anyway. A large one hits Earth every 500,000 years or so.

52 In 1996, a space probe called NEAR Shoemaker was launched to study an asteroid called Eros. It orbited Eros for a year, collecting information, and then did something it wasn't designed to do – it landed on the asteroid. Controllers on Earth slowly lowered its orbit until it touched down. It's still there today.

▲ This is NEAR Shoemaker's last image of Eros. The bottom of the picture is blurred, because the signal was lost as the spacecraft touched down.

53 Asteroids contain valuable minerals such as gold and platinum. One day, these rare minerals will run out on Earth, so there are plans to send spacecraft to asteroids to extract them.

QUIZ

1. How big is Ceres, the biggest asteroid?
2. What does the word 'asteroid' mean?
3. Which asteroid did the NEAR Shoemaker space probe land on?

Answers:
1. 950 kilometres across
2. Star-like 3. Eros

Giant gas planet

54 **Jupiter is the Solar System's biggest planet.** It is 11 times the size of Earth. Jupiter, along with Saturn, Uranus and Neptune, are known as gas giants, because they are huge planets made of gas and liquid.

55 **Jupiter is made mainly of hydrogen and helium.** Below its atmosphere, gas is compressed (squashed) so much that it changes to liquid. Deeper still it is compressed even more, causing the liquid to behave like metal. As Jupiter spins, this liquid metal creates a magnetic field, which is the strongest in the Solar System. At the centre there is thought to be a small, rocky core.

▶ Astronauts will never land on Jupiter, or any other gas giant, because there is no solid surface to touch down on.

Jupiter's thin atmosphere consists of layers of ammonia ice-clouds and water ice

Strong winds churn up many storms in Jupiter's atmosphere, like the Great Red Spot

Atmosphere

Hydrogen gas

Liquid hydrogen and helium

Metallic hydrogen and helium

Core

◀ Jupiter has a dense core about the size of Earth, surrounded by liquid and gas.

Powerful winds blow Jupiter's clouds into wide, light and dark-coloured bands

Fact file: JUPITER

Named after: The king of the Roman gods

Diameter: 142,984 kilometres (11.2 times Earth)

Distance from the Sun: 779 million kilometres

Time to spin once: 9.9 hours

Time to orbit the Sun: 11.9 years

Average temperature: -110°C

Number of moons: 67

Temperatures at the tops of the clouds are around -110°C, but the temperature increases deeper in the atmosphere

56 It takes less than ten hours for Jupiter to spin once. This is faster than any other planet in the Solar System, and even causes Jupiter to bulge in the middle.

57 The Great Red Spot is a permanent storm in Jupiter's atmosphere. It is a vast hurricane, much larger than Earth. The storm has been raging for hundreds of years.

I DON'T BELIEVE IT!

Jupiter is made of the same material as a star, so if it had carried on growing and gained enough mass, it could have become the Solar System's second star.

Jupiter's moons

58 Jupiter has more moons than any other planet. This is because of its huge size, as it means it has a very strong pull of gravity. So far, 67 moons have been discovered. The four biggest can be seen with binoculars. They're known as the Galilean moons, because they were seen for the first time by the Italian astronomer, Galileo Galilei, in 1610.

▲ Through a pair of binoculars, Jupiter's Galilean moons look like a line of stars alongside the planet.

59 The Galilean moons were a surprise for astronomers. These icy worlds all have very different features, and are not the dead, dusty worlds that scientists expected them to be.

▼ The Galilean moons were the first of Jupiter's moons to be discovered, and the first moons found orbiting another planet.

SPOTTING JUPITER
You will need:
a pair of binoculars

On a clear night, find the brightest 'star' in the sky. Look at it through your binoculars. If it has a line of tiny dots of light on one or both sides, you've found Jupiter – and its Galilean moons.

Io

Europa

Ganymede

Callisto

60 Jupiter's largest moon, Ganymede, is also the biggest in the Solar System. It is 1.5 times the size of our Moon. Ganymede is covered with a deep layer of ice. The second largest, Callisto, is the most heavily cratered object in the Solar System.

61 Io is the Solar System's most volcanically active moon. More than 150 volcanoes spew yellow, red and black sulphur onto its surface. One of its volcanoes, Loki, gives out more heat than all of Earth's active volcanoes combined.

▼ Volcanoes shoot plumes of sulphur up to 300 kilometres above Io.

63 Four of Jupiter's smaller moons circle the gas giant within Io's orbit. They are called Metis, Adrastea, Amalthea and Thebe. All are odd shapes, as they don't have the mass needed to form a round, circular shape.

62 Europa is covered with unusually smooth ice. Scientists think the ice may be floating on an ocean of water, which is kept from freezing by the heat inside Europa. This ocean could be around 100 kilometres deep, and could contain life if conditions are right. In the future, probes may explore Europa's ocean for signs of life.

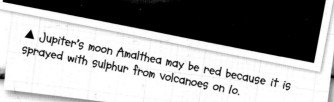

▲ Jupiter's moon Amalthea may be red because it is sprayed with sulphur from volcanoes on Io.

Remarkable rings

64 **Saturn is the Solar System's second biggest planet.** It is surrounded by huge, shining rings. Like Jupiter, Saturn is made almost completely of hydrogen and helium. Below its thin atmosphere, these gases are compressed so much that they become liquid.

Saturn gets its colour from sulphur in its atmosphere

The total width of Saturn's rings is about three-quarters of the distance from Earth to the Moon, but they are only a few hundred metres thick

▶ Saturn spins so fast that it bulges outwards at the middle.

65 **Millions of ice particles make up Saturn's rings.** This is what makes them so bright. They orbit the planet like tiny moons reflecting sunlight. The rings are thought to be the remains of destroyed moons, comets or asteroids.

The fierce winds blowing in Saturn's atmosphere form faint bands across its surface

◀ The ice in Saturn's rings ranges in size from specks smaller than a grain of sand to huge chunks.

66 Like the other gas giants, Saturn's upper atmosphere blows around the planet in bands. This means that gas is moved around at high speed, forming huge storms. Saturn is home to many storms, including vast hurricanes at its poles.

▲ The *Cassini* spacecraft spotted this hurricane at Saturn's North Pole in 2012, rotating at the centre of a huge, six-sided storm. This image has been coloured to show different cloud heights.

67 If you could find a big enough bath of water, Saturn would float in it. This is because despite its huge size, it has the lowest density of all the planets.

Gaps and bends in the rings are caused by the pull of gravity from nearby moons

Fact file: SATURN

Named after: The Roman god of agriculture
Diameter: 120,536 kilometres (9.5 times Earth)
Distance from the Sun: 1434 million kilometres
Time to spin once: 10.7 hours
Time to orbit the Sun: 29.4 years
Average temperature: -140°C
Number of moons: 62

I DON'T BELIEVE IT!
When Galileo first looked at Saturn through his telescope in 1610, he mistook the planet's rings for two moons.

Saturn's moons

68 Saturn has nearly as many moons as Jupiter. So far, 62 have been confirmed. Saturn and its moons were explored by the *Cassini* spacecraft, which arrived at Saturn in 2004. It discovered moons that are too small to be seen from Earth.

69 Some of Saturn's moons orbit inside its rings. These are called shepherd moons because they herd the ring particles together, like a shepherd keeping a flock of sheep together. Shepherd moons give Saturn's rings sharper edges.

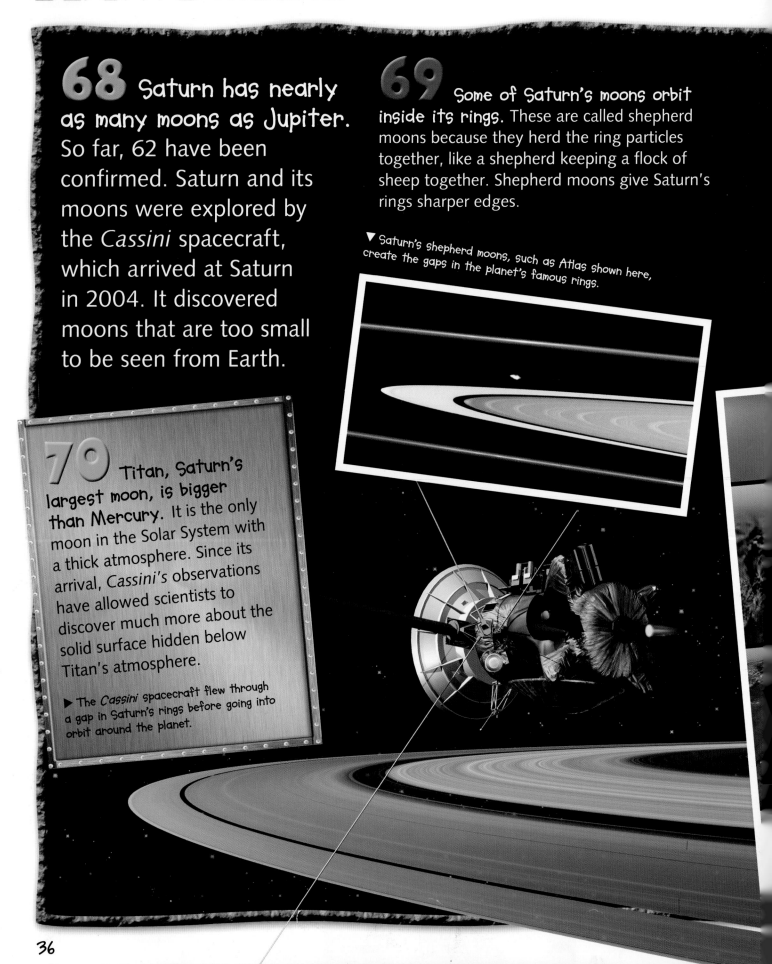

▼ Saturn's shepherd moons, such as Atlas shown here, create the gaps in the planet's famous rings.

70 Titan, Saturn's largest moon, is bigger than Mercury. It is the only moon in the Solar System with a thick atmosphere. Since its arrival, *Cassini*'s observations have allowed scientists to discover much more about the solid surface hidden below Titan's atmosphere.

▶ The *Cassini* spacecraft flew through a gap in Saturn's rings before going into orbit around the planet.

QUIZ

1. Which spacecraft has been exploring Saturn and its moons since 2004?
2. What is the name for the moons that orbit inside Saturn's rings?
3. Which of Saturn's moons is the biggest?

Answers:
1. Cassini 2. Shepherd moons 3. Titan

71 The European Space Agency landed a mini-probe called *Huygens* on Titan in 2005. It was carried to Saturn by the *Cassini* spacecraft. *Huygens* found lakes on Titan, but instead of water they're filled with chemicals including ethane and methane. *Huygens* also carried a microphone that picked up the sound of wind blowing on the moon. This was the first sound ever recorded on another planetary body.

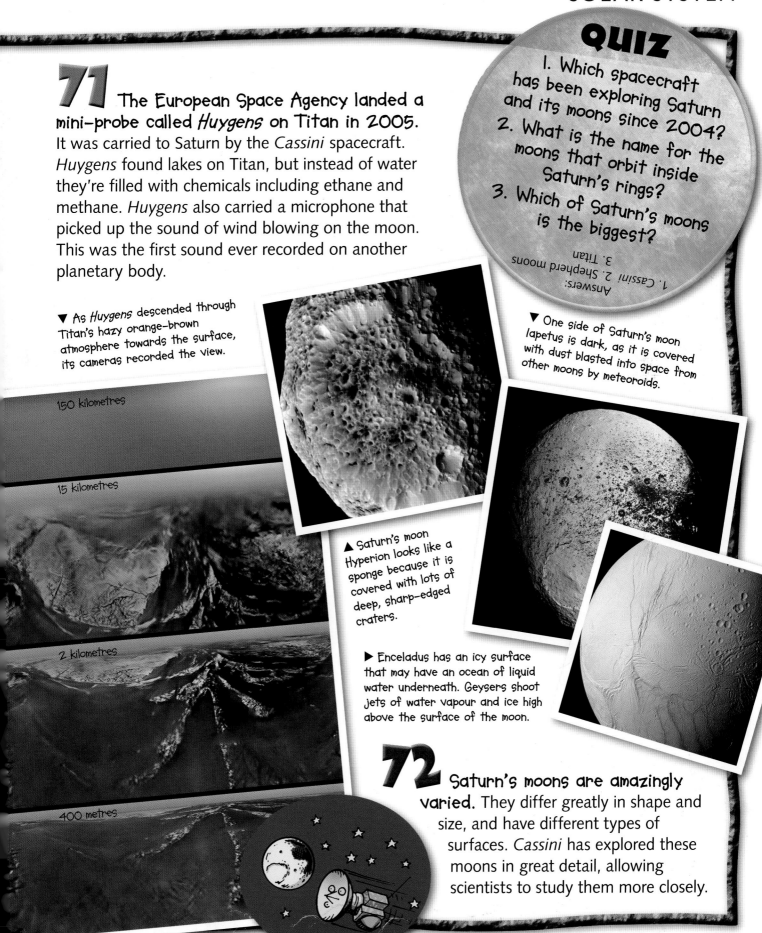

▼ As *Huygens* descended through Titan's hazy orange-brown atmosphere towards the surface, its cameras recorded the view.

150 kilometres

15 kilometres

2 kilometres

400 metres

▼ One side of Saturn's moon Iapetus is dark, as it is covered with dust blasted into space from other moons by meteoroids.

▲ Saturn's moon Hyperion looks like a sponge because it is covered with lots of deep, sharp-edged craters.

▶ Enceladus has an icy surface that may have an ocean of liquid water underneath. Geysers shoot jets of water vapour and ice high above the surface of the moon.

72 Saturn's moons are amazingly varied. They differ greatly in shape and size, and have different types of surfaces. *Cassini* has explored these moons in great detail, allowing scientists to study them more closely.

A blue-green world

73 Uranus, the seventh planet from the Sun, is about four times bigger than Earth. It has an atmosphere of hydrogen and helium. Below it is an ocean of liquid water, ammonia and methane surrounding a rocky core.

Dark, dusty rings

74 Unlike the other planets, Uranus spins on its side. This means that one pole faces the Sun for 42 years and then the other pole faces the Sun for 42 years. Scientists think that Uranus may have been knocked onto its side when an Earth-sized object crashed into it while it was forming.

▲ Uranus has 13 rings. They reflect less light than Saturn's rings, so are not as easily seen.

I DON'T BELIEVE IT!

When Uranus was discovered in 1781, it was almost named *Georgium Sidus* (Georgian planet) after King George III of Great Britain. Uranus was instead chosen, after the ancient Greek god of the sky.

May, 1972:
The *Voyager* multiplanet mission was officially approved, and work began to build *Voyager 2* and its twin, *Voyager I*.

20 August, 1977:

Ariel

Titania

▼ Uranus's five largest moons are Umbriel, Miranda, Oberon, Titania and Ariel.

Oberon

Umbriel

Miranda

75 Uranus has 27 moons. Its biggest moon, Titania, is less than half the size of our Moon. Even though it is so small, it was spotted as long ago as 1787 by the astronomer William Herschel, who also discovered Uranus.

Fact file: URANUS

Named after: The Greek god of the sky
Diameter: 51,118 kilometres (4.0 times Earth)
Distance from the Sun: 2873 million kilometres
Time to spin once: 17.2 hours
Time to orbit the Sun: 83.7 years
Average temperature: -195°C
Number of moons: 27

76 Only one spacecraft has visited Uranus – *Voyager 2*. It left Earth in 1977 and arrived at Uranus 11 years later in 1986. It is still the only spacecraft to have visited all four of the gas giants.

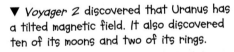
▼ *Voyager 2* discovered that Uranus has a tilted magnetic field. It also discovered ten of its moons and two of its rings.

24 January, 1986: *Voyager 2* made its closest approach to Uranus, coming within 81,500 kilometres of the mysterious planet's cloudtops.

24 January, 1986: Images taken by *Voyager 2* revealed that Uranus's moon Miranda is actually covered in features such as craters, mountains, valleys and ridges.

25 August, 1989: *Voyager 2* reached Neptune, gathering important data about the eighth planet.

The farthest planet

77 The last of the Solar System's eight planets is Neptune. It is the smallest of the gas giants, but still nearly four times bigger than Earth. Like Uranus, it is an icy world made of hydrogen and helium, as well as water, ammonia and methane.

78 Neptune was the first planet found by mathematics. Astronomers noticed that Uranus was being tugged by the gravity of another large body, which affected its orbit. Calculations showed astronomers where to look, and in 1846, Neptune was found.

Fact file: NEPTUNE

Named after: The Roman god of the sea
Diameter: 49,528 kilometres (3.9 times Earth)
Distance from the Sun: 4495 million kilometres
Time to spin once: 16.1 hours
Time to orbit the Sun: 164 years
Average temperature: -200°C
Number of moons: 14

Dark storms in Neptune's atmosphere come and go every few years

Great Dark Spot

▶ Neptune's blue colour is caused by methane in its atmosphere.

▼ Clouds on Earth are made of water, but Neptune's clouds are made of chemicals including methane, ammonia and hydrogen sulphide.

79 Neptune's winds are the fastest in the Solar System. They race around Neptune at almost 2400 kilometres an hour. It is thought that heat bubbling up from Neptune's core creates these winds. Neptune's surface is also streaked with clouds, high in the atmosphere.

▲ Neptune's Great Dark Spot was a giant super-storm spinning anti-clockwise once every 16 days.

80 When *Voyager 2* photographed Neptune in 1989, it captured a large dark storm as big as Earth. The storm was called the Great Dark Spot. But when the Hubble Space Telescope was turned towards Neptune in 1994, the Great Dark Spot had disappeared.

81 Neptune has 14 moons, four of which are shepherd moons. The biggest, Triton, was discovered just 17 days after Neptune itself. Triton is so cold that it has ice volcanoes shooting out a mixture of liquid nitrogen, methane and dust.

▶ Triton's surface is covered with frozen nitrogen, a gas found on Earth.

I DON'T BELIEVE IT!

Neptune was discovered to be a planet in 1846, but it was first seen by the great astronomer, Galileo Galilei, 234 years earlier. Galileo thought he was looking at a star, not a planet.

Distant travellers

82 A comet is a mountain of rock and ice orbiting the Sun. Most comets are too far away for us to see, but occasionally they come closer to the Sun. The Sun's heat changes some of the ice into gas. Gas and dust flying off the comet form long, bright tails.

▼ The cloud or coma around a comet is made of dust and gas. Dust forms one of the comet's tails and gas forms a second tail.

Gas tail

Nucleus

Coma

Dust tail

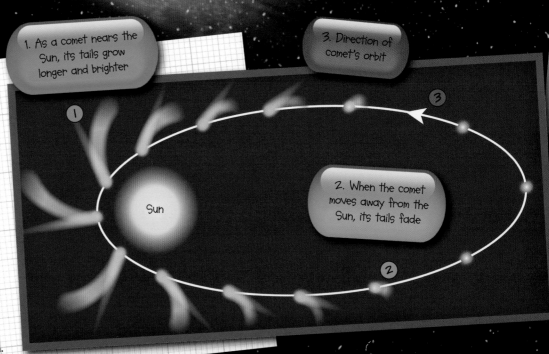

1. As a comet nears the Sun, its tails grow longer and brighter

3. Direction of comet's orbit

Sun

2. When the comet moves away from the Sun, its tails fade

83 A comet's tails always point away from the Sun. Sunlight and particles streaming away from the Sun – called the solar wind – sweep the tails back, away from the Sun.

▶ A comet's tails can be longer than the distance from the Earth to the Sun.

84

In 1994, a comet slammed into the giant planet Jupiter. The comet was called Shoemaker-Levy 9. As it headed for Jupiter, it broke up. One after another, the pieces of the comet hurtled into Jupiter's atmosphere at more than 200 times the speed of a jet airliner, creating fireballs and huge dust clouds.

▶ Pieces of Shoemaker Levy 9 head for Jupiter like a string of pearls.

85

The whole Solar System may be surrounded by millions of comets! Scientists think that some of the comets we see come from a vast cloud of icy rocks that surrounds the entire Solar System. It's called the Oort Cloud. Others come from a closer region outside Neptune, called the Kuiper Belt.

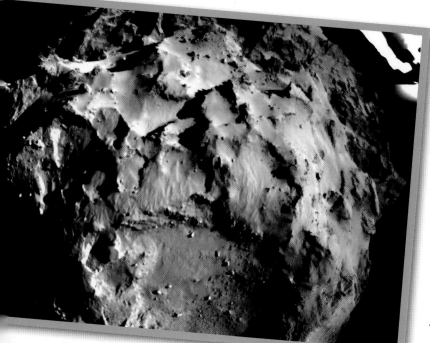

▲ Comet 67P appears in the sky every 6-7 years. On 12th November 2014, the European Space Agency's *Rosetta* spacecraft made history by landing a probe, *Philae*, on the comet. This image was taken by *Philae* during its descent.

I DON'T BELIEVE IT!

A 'star' with a long tail appeared just before the Battle of Hastings in 1066. It was actually a comet. The English King, Harold II, thought it was a sign of bad luck. He was right — he lost the battle!

86

The comets we see from time to time spend only a tiny part of their orbit near the Sun. The rest of the time, their long, thin orbit takes them far away to the outer reaches of the Solar System. These can take thousands of years to orbit the Sun. Some comets get caught up in much smaller orbits and appear every few years.

Dwarf planets

NAME	DIAMETER (KILOMETRES)	DISCOVERED	NUMBER OF MOONS
PLUTO	2368	1930	5
ERIS	2326	2005	1
MAKEMAKE	1430	2005	0
HAUMEA	1240	2004	2
CERES	950	1801	0

▲ These are the first five dwarf planets to be officially recognized. More discoveries are certain to follow.

87 Dwarf planets are small worlds orbiting the Sun that are not big enough to be classed as planets. There are five 'official' dwarf planets, but dozens more have been found and may soon join the dwarf planet club.

88 Pluto was a planet for 76 years. When Pluto was discovered in 1930, it became the Solar System's ninth planet. But when astronomers started finding more smaller worlds like Pluto, they decided to call them dwarf planets. So in 2006, Pluto became a dwarf planet. Pluto's orbit is oval-shaped, sometimes crossing inside Neptune's orbit.

▼ Ceres takes less than five years to orbit the Sun. Eris, much further away, takes 557 years.

Haumea

Eris

▶ Dwarf planet Pluto has five moons. The biggest is called Charon. A spacecraft called *New Horizons* will arrive at Pluto in 2015 to study the dwarf planet and its moons for the first time.

▶ Even though it is so far away, Makemake reflects just enough sunlight to be seen by large telescopes on Earth.

Ceres may have a deep layer of ice under its thin, dusty crust.

Makemake

Ceres

Pluto

89 Only one dwarf planet has been found in the Asteroid Belt between Mars and Jupiter. It's called Ceres, and it is also classed as the largest asteroid. The other dwarf planets orbit the Sun in the Kuiper Belt, beyond the farthest planets.

90 Eris' discovery made astronomers rethink Pluto's status as a planet. Eris has more mass than Pluto, so both were classed as dwarf planets. Eris is the most distant dwarf planet, made of rock and ice.

▲ Eris has a tiny moon called Dysnomia. In Greek mythology, Dysnomia was the daughter of the Greek god Eris.

QUIZ

1. When was Pluto discovered?
2. Which dwarf planet is bigger than Pluto?
3. Which dwarf planet is further from the Sun — Haumea or Makemake?

Answers:
1. 1930 2. Eris 3. Makemake

▶ Haumea may have been set spinning very fast when something crashed into it millions of years ago.

91 Dwarf planet Haumea is a very strange shape. It spins so fast, once every four hours, that it has stretched out into the shape of an American football. Further out from Haumea, Makemake's surface has large amounts of solid frozen methane, found as a gas on Earth.

The search for life

92 Before the space age, some people thought intelligent creatures lived on Mars. So far, life has not been found on Mars or anywhere else in the Solar System, but scientists are still searching.

93 Two *Viking* spacecraft landed on Mars in 1976 to look for signs of life. When they tested the Martian soil, the results seemed to show signs of microscopic living organisms. However, scientists decided that the chemical activity found was not evidence of Martian life. In 2013, the *Curiosity* rover found evidence in Gale Crater of an environment that could have supported microscopic life billions of years ago.

▼ The *Curiosity* rover landed in Gale Crater on Mars on 6 August, 2012.

◀ When *Viking 2* landed on Mars in 1976, its cameras looked out on a rock-strewn part of the planet called Utopian Plain.

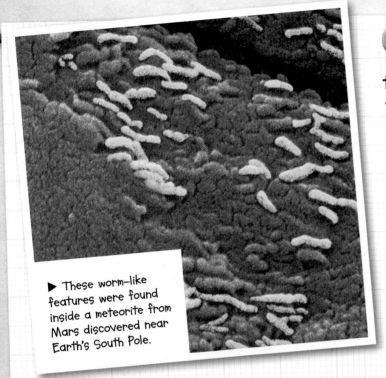

► These worm-like features were found inside a meteorite from Mars discovered near Earth's South Pole.

94 In 1996, scientists thought they may have finally found signs of Martian life. They discovered worm-like features in a meteorite from Mars that looked like microscopic fossils of bacteria. But other scientists disagreed. It will take more exploration to know for definite if life ever existed on Mars.

95 Life in the Solar System was previously thought to only be possible in a narrow band called the 'Goldilocks Zone'. But now scientists think life could exist elsewhere. One of the most promising possibilities is Jupiter's moon Europa, where there is thought to be an ocean of water underneath its icy surface.

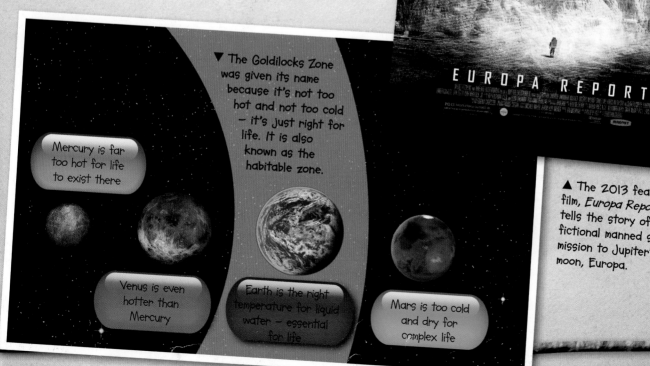

FEAR. SACRIFICE. CONTACT.

EUROPA REPORT

▼ The Goldilocks Zone was given its name because it's not too hot and not too cold – it's just right for life. It is also known as the habitable zone.

Mercury is far too hot for life to exist there

Venus is even hotter than Mercury

Earth is the right temperature for liquid water – essential for life

Mars is too cold and dry for complex life

▲ The 2013 feature film, *Europa Report*, tells the story of a fictional manned space mission to Jupiter's moon, Europa.

The Solar System's Future

96 In the distant future, the Moon will look much smaller to our descendants. This is because its orbit is slowly increasing in size, moving it away from Earth. Every year the Moon moves about 3.8 centimetres further away from us.

▼ High tides on Earth are speeding up the Moon, causing it to move further away from Earth.

▶ The Moon is slowly spiralling away from Earth.

Key

(1) The Moon's gravity raises a bulge of water on Earth

(2) The spinning Earth drags the water ahead of the Moon

(3) The water pulls on the Moon, speeding it up and increasing its orbit

Moon's orbit

Earth's rotation

QUIZ

1. How much further from Earth will the Moon be ten years from now?
2. What colour will the Sun be when it swells up?
3. What kind of star will the Sun finally become?

Answers:
1. 38 centimetres 2. Red 3. A white dwarf

97 The Sun is gradually growing bigger and brighter. This is because the amount of hydrogen gas in the Sun is decreasing over time. In about a billion years, it will begin to evaporate Earth's oceans.

98 In about four billion years, a galactic collision will take place. The Milky Way galaxy that includes our Solar System will collide with neighbouring Andromeda galaxy, although Earth and the Solar System should survive.

◀ When the Milky Way and Andromeda galaxies meet, they will merge together to form one enormous new galaxy.

99 About five billion years from now, the Sun will run out of hydrogen and other fuels it needs. Nuclear fusion will stop. The Sun will swell up into a massive red giant star and cool down.

▶ The red giant Sun will be over 200 times bigger than the Sun today – big enough to swallow the closest planets, perhaps including Earth.

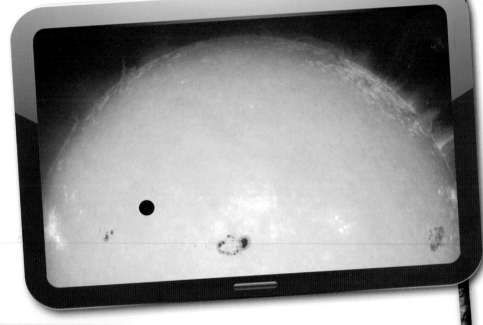

100 The red giant star will eventually blow away its outer layers of gas. This will leave a glowing halo of gas around the star. The remaining star will then shrink to become a tiny white dwarf. The white dwarf will cool and fade away over billions of years.

◀ The cloud of gas that will surround the shrinking Sun is called a planetary nebula.

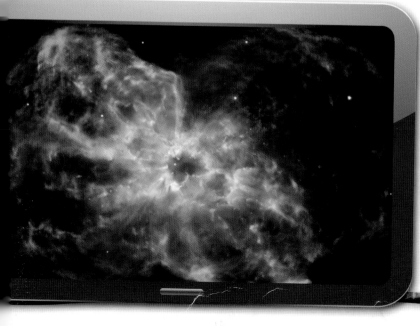

49

STARS AND GALAXIES

101 Stars are giant balls of very hot gas. These give off lots of heat as well as light, which allow us to see them in the sky. The stars we see at night are just a tiny fraction of the number found in the Universe. The National Observatory in London, UK estimates that there are around 70,000 million million million stars in the Universe.

▼ Stars are grouped together in large collections called galaxies. This image is part of the Large Magellanic Cloud, a neighbouring galaxy to our own galaxy, the Milky Way.

When it all began

102 The Universe is approximately 13.7 billion (thousand million) years old. If you squeezed down that time into a single 24-hour day, then the very first people on Earth didn't appear until the last minute.

103 Scientists believe the Universe began out of a single point. The theory of how the Universe began is often called the Big Bang, but it wasn't an explosion. Scientists believe that everything expanded out of a single point.

13.7 BILLION YEARS AGO

▲ Inflation from a single point was rapid with the Universe doubling its size at least a hundred times in a fraction of a second.

CREATE A UNIVERSE
You will need:
marker pen   a balloon
1. Blow the balloon up a bit and hold the neck so no air escapes.
2. Mark some small circles on its surface with the pen. Think of each circle as a galaxy.
3. Blow the balloon up slowly to its full size. The galaxies will get further and further apart as the balloon expands.

13.5 BILLION YEARS AGO

▲ Cosmic background radiation from the Big Bang is given out.

▲ The Universe continues to expand as the earliest stars form.

104 The first stars didn't form until 200 million years after the Big Bang. Millions more followed including our Sun, which formed almost 9 thousand million years later.

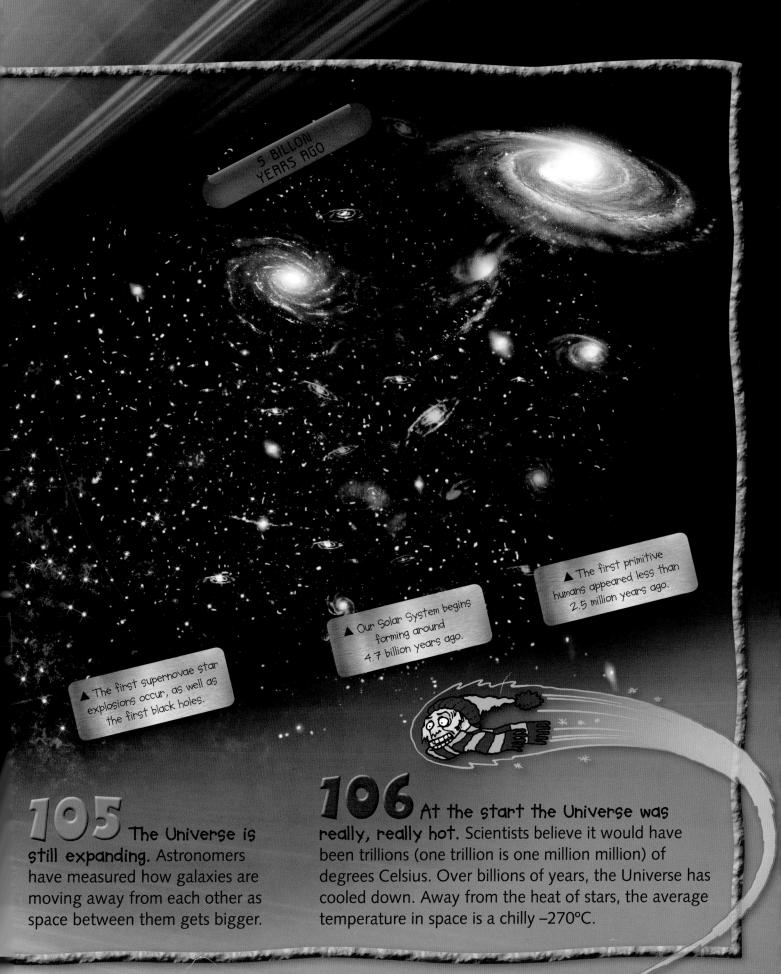

5 BILLION YEARS AGO

▲ The first supernovae star explosions occur, as well as the first black holes.

▲ Our Solar System begins forming around 4.7 billion years ago.

▲ The first primitive humans appeared less than 2.5 million years ago.

105 The Universe is still expanding. Astronomers have measured how galaxies are moving away from each other as space between them gets bigger.

106 At the start the Universe was really, really hot. Scientists believe it would have been trillions (one trillion is one million million) of degrees Celsius. Over billions of years, the Universe has cooled down. Away from the heat of stars, the average temperature in space is a chilly −270°C.

Universal matters

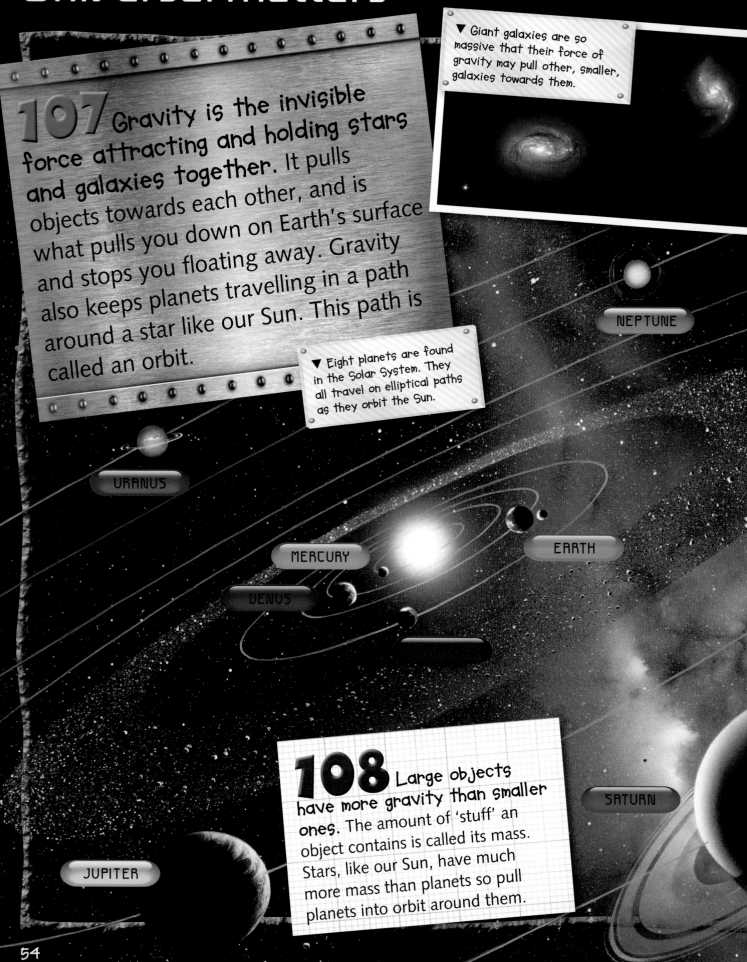

107 Gravity is the invisible force attracting and holding stars and galaxies together. It pulls objects towards each other, and is what pulls you down on Earth's surface and stops you floating away. Gravity also keeps planets travelling in a path around a star like our Sun. This path is called an orbit.

▼ Giant galaxies are so massive that their force of gravity may pull other, smaller, galaxies towards them.

▼ Eight planets are found in the Solar System. They all travel on elliptical paths as they orbit the Sun.

NEPTUNE

URANUS

MERCURY

EARTH

VENUS

108 Large objects have more gravity than smaller ones. The amount of 'stuff' an object contains is called its mass. Stars, like our Sun, have much more mass than planets so pull planets into orbit around them.

JUPITER

SATURN

NEAREST STARS TO EARTH

Proxima Centauri	4.2 light years
Alpha Cen A	4.4 light years
Alpha Cen B	4.4 light years
Barnard's Star	6.0 light years
CN Leo	7.8 light years

► Gaia satellite will measure how far away one billion stars are.

109 Light travels incredibly fast – at speeds of almost 299,792,458 metres per second. It can travel more than seven times around Earth in just a second. Scientists use the distance that light travels in one year to measure the huge distances in space. A single light year is 63,000 times the distance between Earth and the Sun.

110 Launched in 2013, the Gaia satellite will measure how far away stars are from Earth. It is on a five-year mission and will build up a 3D map, measuring some of the stars' distances to within 0.001% accuracy.

111 When we view distant objects in the Universe, we are seeing how they looked in the past. Even though light travels really fast, it can take millions of years to reach us from a distant star or galaxy. What we see is how the object looked millions of years ago.

DISTANCE LIGHT TRAVELS IN KILOMETRES

1 light second	299,792.5 km
1 light minute	17.98 million km
1 light day	25.9 billion km
1 light year	9.46 million million km

► Our Sun is our closest star at 149,600,000 km away. The next nearest star is Proxima Centauri. It is 4.2 light years away.

I DON'T BELIEVE IT!

In just over three years, Hipparcos – a satellite launched by ESA in 1989 – measured how far over a million different stars were from Earth.

Star nurseries

112 Stars are born in giant star nurseries called nebulae. Nebulae are giant clouds containing dust and gases, mostly hydrogen and some helium. Inside a nebula are all the elements needed to form new stars, called protostars.

▼ A single nebula can contain thousands of new stars. In 2005, the Spitzer telescope discovered 150 protostars never seen before in this Trifid Nebula.

113 There may be as many as 2500 nebulae in the Milky Way. Over the centuries, many astronomers have spotted nebulae. Brother and sister, William and Caroline Herschel performed a major search of the skies in the late 18th and early 19th centuries.

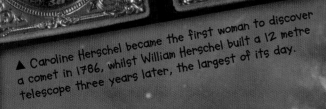

▲ Caroline Herschel became the first woman to discover a comet in 1786, whilst William Herschel built a 12 metre telescope three years later, the largest of its day.

114 An emission nebula is a bright nebula full of shining stars. We can see the Horsehead Nebula's dark clouds because another, brighter emission nebula is behind, surrounding it with light.

115 Nebulae are often vast. The Orion nebula is one of the nearest to Earth. It measures about 30 light years across. Other nebulae are even bigger. It would take light over 600 years, for example, to cross the giant Tarantula Nebula.

116 The Cat's Eye Nebula is a planetary nebula. These different types of cloud exist around some dying stars. The Cat's Eye Nebula has at least 11 surrounding rings of gas.

The Horsehead Nebula is found in the Orion constellation and is 1500 light years from Earth.

The Tarantula Nebula is about 160,000 light years from Earth and is packed full of young stars.

The Cat's Eye nebula was discovered by William Herschel in 1786 and lies around 3000 light years away.

QUIZ

1. How wide in light years is the Orion Nebula?
2. Which is the most common gas in a nebula?
3. In which nebula were 150 young stars discovered in 2005?

Answers:
1. 30 2. Hydrogen
3. Trifid nebula

Birth of a star

Clumps of gas in this nebula start to shrink into the tight round balls that will become stars.

117 New stars, called protostars, form from clouds of gas and dust in a nebula. The dust and gas gets drawn together and becomes hotter and more dense. As the clump gets bigger and more tightly packed, its gravity increases. This force pulls in yet more dust and gas.

The gas spirals round as it is pulled inwards. Any left-over gas and dust may form planets around the new star.

▼ The centre of the NGC 4214 galaxy contains hundreds of hot, young stars being formed. Many of these are less than two million years old.

Deep in its centre, the new star starts making energy, but it is still hidden by the cloud of dust and gas.

The dust and gas are blown away and we can see the star shining. Maybe it has a family of planets like the Sun.

118 A protostar can take 100,000 years to form. During this time, the clump grows and grows, drawing in more material. The middle of the clump is squeezed more and more tightly together so that it gets incredibly hot and pressurised.

119 Stars turn hydrogen gas into helium and energy. If the centre of a protostar gets hot enough, it will start nuclear fusion reactions, which use hydrogen as their fuel.

▼ NASA's Wide-field Infrared Survey Explorer (WISE) satellite has captured a multitude of stars and galaxies, including a brown dwarf (circled).

120 Some protostars never become proper stars because they don't get big enough. Instead, they gradually cool down and become a failed star, called a brown dwarf.

121 The coolest known star in the Universe is as cold as the North Pole on Earth. A brown dwarf, WISE J085510.83-071442.5 is estimated at –48°C to –13°C.

▲ This artist's impression shows a Y dwarf – a member of the brown dwarf family. They give off little heat and light, so are very hard to find in space.

I DON'T BELIEVE IT!
The core of a protostar needs to be 10 million°C before nuclear reactions occur – that's hot!

Fierce furnaces

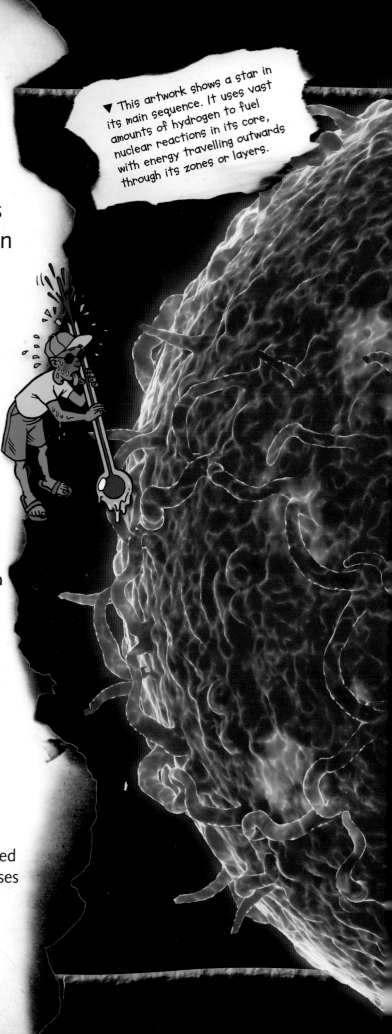

▼ This artwork shows a star in its main sequence. It uses vast amounts of hydrogen to fuel nuclear reactions in its core, with energy travelling outwards through its zones or layers.

122 Stars are enormous furnaces generating vast amounts of energy. In a star's centre, or core, lots of hydrogen gas is used to fuel powerful nuclear fusion reactions.

123 The temperature in a star's core during its main sequence is unbelievably hot, about 15 million°C. As a star nears the end of its life, the temperature in the core may increase.

124 Nine out of ten stars spotted in the night sky burn hydrogen to form helium. These stars are in their main sequence – the period in the life of a star after it has developed from a protostar. The main sequence lasts until the star runs out of hydrogen. The Sun is roughly halfway through its nine to ten billion year-long main sequence.

125 Two forces keep the star approximately the same size during its main sequence. The incredibly hot gas heated by the fusion reactions in the star's core presses outwards with huge force. This pressure is balanced by the star's gravity pulling gas in towards its centre.

126 Energy from the core of a star can take thousands of years to reach its surface. It journeys through the star's zones by either radiation or convection. In radiation, the energy travels in waves, like light. In convection, the energy travels on currents inside the star, a bit like really hot wind.

Energy moves outwards

Gravity pushes inwards

Radiative zone

Core

Photosphere

QUIZ

1. What is the centre of a star called?
2. Is the Sun at the end of its life or in its main sequence?
3. Does energy travel in waves via convection or radiation?

Answers:
1. The core
2. The Sun is in its main sequence
3. Radiation

Shining bright

127 Sirius is the brightest star in our night sky. It glows 25 times more brightly than the Sun, and is just 8.6 light years away – one of the closest stars to Earth. Scientists use a measurement called apparent magnitude to gauge how bright stars appear to us on Earth.

128 Some stars that appear to shine dimly are actually very bright. They are just a long distance away from us. Rigel, for example, shines about 100,000 times more brightly than the Sun, but is located 770 light years away.

▶ Three of the four telescopes that make up the Very Large Telescope (VLT) in Chile's Atacama Desert.

▼ Some of the brightest stars in the southern Milky Way as seen from Earth, can be spotted in this view at dawn over Chile.

Sirius

Canopus

Large Magellanic Cloud

Carina Nebula

Alpha and Beta Centauri

129 Stars can form distinctive patterns in the night sky called asterisms. These stars may look as if they are all the same distance from us, but they're not. The farthest star in the Big Dipper, Alkaid, is three times farther away than the nearest, Megrez.

Dubhe
Merak
Megrez
Phecda
Alioth
Alkaid
Mizar

▲ The Big Dipper seen in the Northern hemisphere is made up of seven stars that are different distances from Earth.

THE BRIGHTEST STARS FROM EARTH	DISTANCE FROM EARTH	APPARENT MAGNITUDE
Our Sun	149,600,000 km	-26.72
Sirius	8.6 light years away	-1.46
Canopus	310 light years away	-0.72
Rigil Kentaurus	4.3 light years away	-0.27
Arcturus	34 light years away	-0.04

See page 11 for a light year conversion to kilometres.

130 Some stars vary how brightly they shine. These are known as intrinsic variable stars. One type, called Cephid variables, change their brightness in regular cycles lasting just days or weeks.

131 Most stars do not twinkle in the sky. They give off a steady light, but appear to twinkle because of moving air in Earth's atmosphere. This bends and twists the light, giving the impression of twinkling.

I DON'T BELIEVE IT!
The giant star Eta Carinae shines over one million times more brightly than the Sun.

▲ Discovered in 2002, V838 Monocerotis is a variable star that sometimes shines 600,000 times more brightly than the Sun.

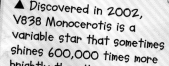

Dwarfs and giants

132 Astronomers group stars together in different ways, including by size. At one end of the size scale are hypergiants and supergiants, like Antares. These stars can be 100 times bigger than the Sun and have relatively short lives because they burn their fuel so quickly.

133 The most common type of stars are red dwarfs. They are less than half the size of the Sun and make up over two thirds of all stars. They burn their fuel more slowly than stars like the Sun, so they last as long as a trillion years.

Name: Antares
Spectral Type: M
Temp: Cool
Size: Red supergiant

Name: Rigel A
Spectral Type: B
Temp: Hot
Size: Blue giant

Name: Sirius A
Spectral Type: A
Temp: Hot
Size: Blue dwarf

134 Astronomers also group stars together by temperature. You may be used to thinking of blue for cold and red for hot, but the hottest stars, like Rigel, appear white-blue and the coolest stars look red.

SPECTRAL TYPE	COLOUR	TEMPERATURE
O		28,000–50,000°C
B		10,000–28,000°C
A		7500–10,000°C
F		6000–7500°C
G		5000–6000°C
K		3500–5000°C
M		2500–5500°C

135
The stellar spectral types range from O to M. Type O stars are the hottest with temperatures of 30,000°C or more. The Sun, with a surface temperature of 5500°C, is a type G star – in the middle. Type M stars, like Antares, are the coolest with temperatures below 3500°C.

▲ The Sun, Sirius A and Rigel A are all dwarfed by this massive star, Antares, which has a diameter over 880 times bigger than the Sun's.

Name: The Sun
Spectral Type: G
Temp: Medium
Size: Yellow dwarf

136
The fate of a star depends on its mass. For stars with a mass of more than three times the Sun, the ending is usually violent, involving a swelling in size before exploding as a supernova.

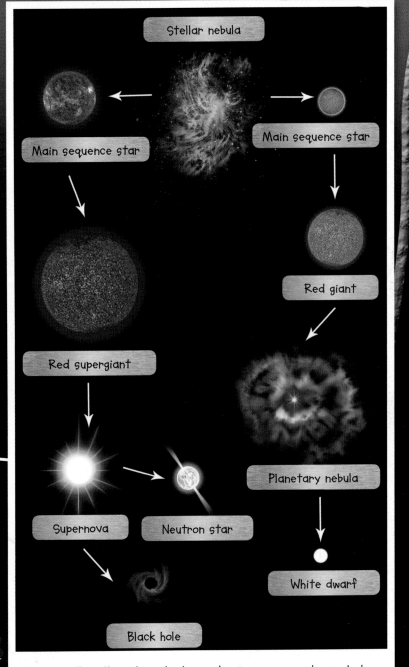

Stellar nebula

Main sequence star

Main sequence star

Red giant

Red supergiant

Planetary nebula

Supernova   Neutron star

White dwarf

Black hole

▲ Stars all go through protostar and main sequence stages, but their mass determines the stages after they run out of hydrogen in their core to use as fuel.

I DON'T BELIEVE IT!
VY Canis Majoris is such a huge hypergiant, it would take over 1000 years in a fast jet aircraft to circle it!

More than one star

137 **Most stars in the Universe are not on their own.** Our Sun is a lone star, but about a third of the stars in the Milky Way are part of a binary (two) or multiple (three plus) star system.

138 **Binary stars are attracted by each other's force of gravity.** The two stars travel round a point, called the centre of mass. This is like the balancing point on a see-saw and is often between the two stars.

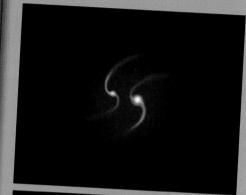

▼ These binary stars orbit around a point between them. As one star is more massive than the other, the centre of mass is closer to it than the smaller star.

MAKE BINARY STARS

You will need:
pencil   piece of string
one large and one small ball of modelling clay

1. Push the balls on each end of the pencil and tie the string around its middle.
2. Dangle the pencil and balls and move the string along the pencil until the two balls balance.
3. Gently push one end of the pencil to see the two stars orbit round. The point where the string is tied is the common centre of mass between the two binary stars.

139 More than 1000 stars can be found in the Pleiades cluster, which is 440 light years away. It is made up of hot, bright, young stars and brown dwarfs, which shine dimly. Many ancient civilizations recognized this star cluster in the night sky.

▶ The Nebra Sky Disc is a 3600-year-old bronze disc found in Germany with gold insets showing the Sun, Moon and stars of the Pleiades cluster.

140 Some stars are found in large groups called open clusters. Many stars may form in the same area of a nebula at around the same time. At first, these stars stay close to each other before gradually drifting away.

◀ Some of the hot, young stars of the Pleiades open cluster shine brightly. Astronomers have found more than 1100 of these clusters in the Milky Way alone.

141 Globular clusters can contain hundreds of thousands of stars. These are large collections of mostly old stars found in the centre of a galaxy. Omega Centauri is a globular cluster containing 10 million stars.

▶ Many of these stars in Omega Centauri are millions of kilometres apart from each other.

Life cycle of a star

142 Stars don't last forever — they die when they run out of fuel. When a star the size of the Sun has used all its hydrogen, it will start using helium in the nuclear reactions at its core, and the star will swell in size to become a red giant.

143 As a red giant cools and shrinks, it becomes a small star called a white dwarf. It is packed tightly with material, but quite small. White dwarfs eventually fade, but can still shine for billions of years.

144 Stars with much lower mass then the Sun will just fizzle out. Once they have run out of hydrogen fuel, they are not big enough to use helium in their reactions, so they dim and cool.

145 There is one enormous dying star that is bigger than the distance from the Sun to Jupiter and back! Mu Cephei (also known as the Garnet Star) shines about 100,000 times more brightly than the Sun.

146 Planetary nebulae are created by some dying stars, but they were named by mistake. When astronomers first spotted them they thought they looked like the gas planets, Jupiter and Neptune. Planetary nebulae contain lots of gas, but no planets.

▲ A dying star blows away layers of dust and gas to form this planetary nebula, called the Helix Nebula.

▶ This chart shows the likely fates of different types of stars found throughout the Universe.

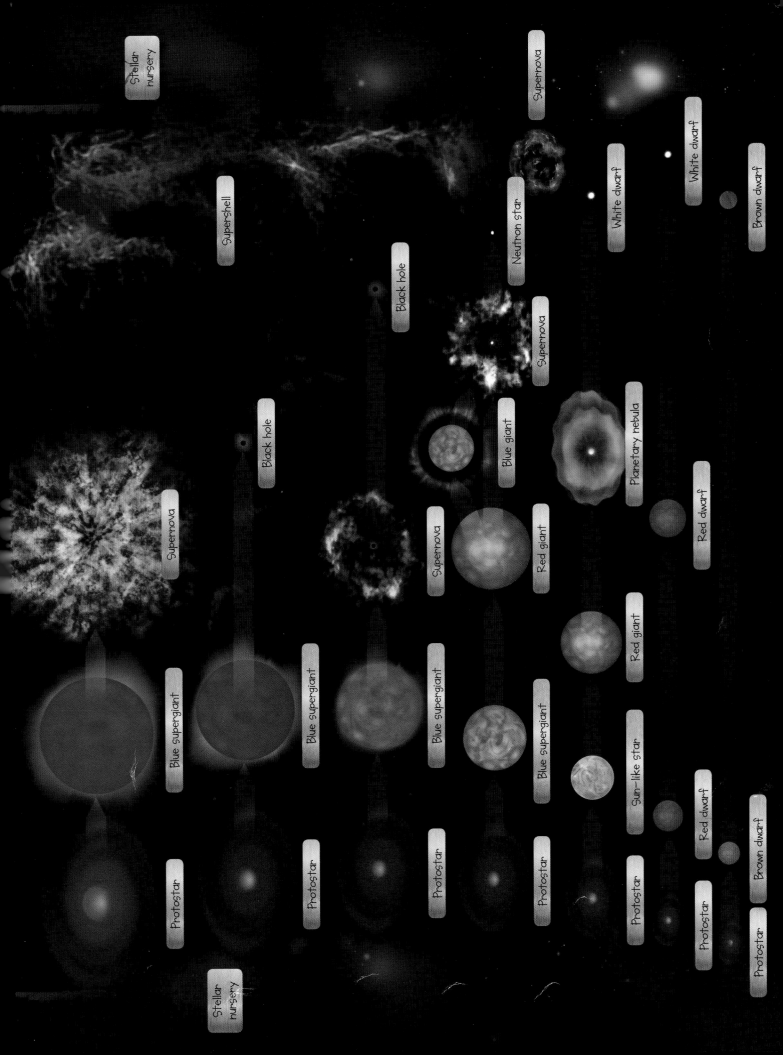

Stunning supernovae

147 Some stars die spectacular and violent deaths through giant explosions. Stars eight or more times more massive than the Sun swell up as they burn all their hydrogen, helium and other elements as fuel. The core of the star collapses in on itself and then much of the star rebounds in a truly gigantic explosion called a supernova.

148 One supernova was so bright, it could be viewed from Earth by day. In 1604, astronomer Johannes Kepler tracked a supernova explosion using just his eyes despite the fact that it was some 20,000 light years away.

▶ Johannes Kepler was able to track his supernova for a full year. Kepler's teacher, Tycho Brahe, had also tracked a supernova in 1572.

◀ This SN1006 supernova remnant is approximately 60 light years in diameter. It is the remains of a white dwarf star, which was ripped apart in a supernova explosion.

I DON'T BELIEVE IT!

Supernovae explosions fling out gas and dust at high speed — as fast as 30,000 kilometres per second.

▼ The Crab Nebula is still expanding at an approximate speed of 1500 km per second.

149 Some supernova remnants can be observed long after the explosion. In 1054, a supernova explosion occurred, which Chinese astronomers called a "guest star". The remains of the supernova, now called the Crab Nebula, can still be seen with a telescope and is about 12 light years wide.

150 The first supernova seen since the invention of the telescope was in 1987. Supernova 1987a occurred in the Large Magellanic Cloud galaxy over 160,000 years ago. Astronomers measured debris from the explosion moving at 30 million kilometres an hour.

151 In 2011, Supernova 2010lt was discovered by a 10-year-old Canadian schoolgirl. Kathryn Aurora Gray was the youngest person ever to discover a supernova.

▶ Kathyrn Aurora Gray (seen here meeting Neil Armstrong) spotted the supernova while looking through images taken by a Canadian telescope.

Neutron stars

152 Some exploding stars leave behind a neutron star. The outer layers of the star blast away, leaving behind an incredibly heavy core. Gravity pulls in surrounding matter and draws the core in on itself, making the star incredibly dense and small. A neutron star's gravity is billions of times stronger than the gravity we experience on Earth.

153 A teaspoon of neutron star might weigh more than one million tonnes. Neutron stars can be about 20–25 kilometres in diameter but can have the mass of two of our Suns.

154 Some neutron stars, called pulsars, spin round thousands of times a minute. Pulsars send out streams of radiation as they rotate. PSR J1748-2446ad, spins 716 times a second – that's 43,000 times per minute!

▲ Some neutron stars may draw in matter from neighbouring stars as well as shooting out long jets of radiation from their centre.

QUIZ

155 Neutron stars can sometimes cause massive energy bursts known as star quakes. They crack their outer surfaces as they move, releasing a burst of energy, which flashes through space. In 2004, neutron star, SGR 1806-20, generated the biggest burst of energy ever measured. In a tenth of a second, it contained as much energy as the Sun gives out in 100,000 years.

QUIZ

1. When was the biggest burst of energy measured from a neutron star?
2. In a neutron star, is gravity thousands, millions or billions times stronger than on Earth?
3. Who discovered the first pulsar?

Answers:
1. 2004 2. Billions
3. Jocelyn Bell Burnell

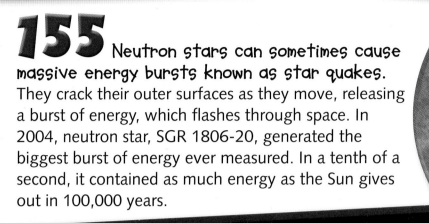

◀ SGR 1806-20 releases energy in a star quake. The star is only 20 kilometres in diameter and spins rapidly completing a full turn every 7.5 seconds.

▼ Pulsar B1919+21 is located approximately 2280 light years from Earth.

156 The first pulsar found was originally called Little Green Men 1. In 1967, a radio astronomer, Jocelyn Bell Burnell, detected a radio signal from space occurring every 1.34 seconds. She called it LGM-1, short for Little Green Men. Instead of being a message from aliens, it turned out to be a pulsar now called PSR B1919+21.

Mysterious black holes

157 Black holes can be formed from the death of massive stars. Stars that have been through a huge supernova still leave a core behind. In some cases, this core collapses in on itself and forms a dense point in space. Astronomers call this a singularity, and it is the centre of a black hole.

158 There's an enormous, mysterious black hole called Sagittarius A* at the middle of our galaxy. Astronomers believe it has the same mass as between three and four million Suns. Supermassive black holes, like Sagittarius A*, are found in the centre of galaxies. The black hole at the centre of the NGC 1277 galaxy is one of the biggest. Scientists estimate its mass to be equal to 17 billion Suns.

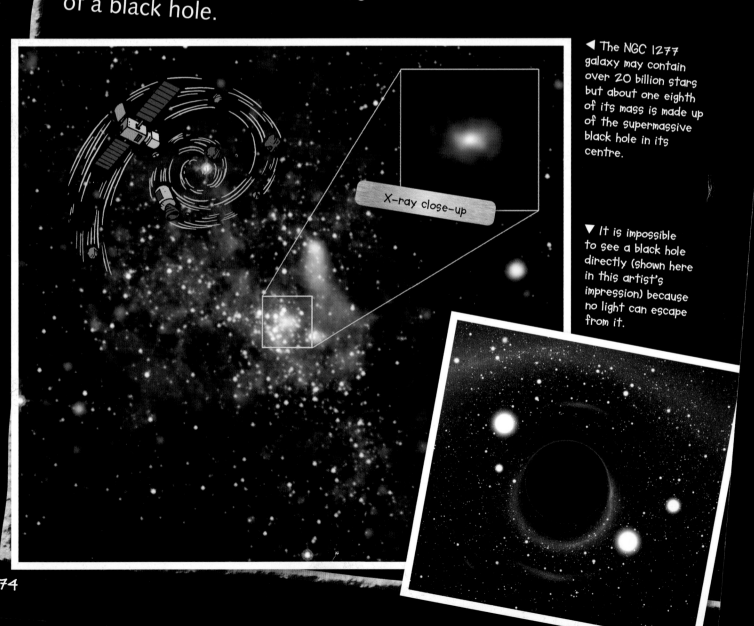

X-ray close-up

◀ The NGC 1277 galaxy may contain over 20 billion stars but about one eighth of its mass is made up of the supermassive black hole in its centre.

▼ It is impossible to see a black hole directly (shown here in this artist's impression) because no light can escape from it.

▲ A Sun–like star plunges towards a supermassive black hole.

159 Nothing can escape a black hole because its gravity is so strong. Matter drawn towards it, including planets and stars, passes the event horizon, a point from which it is impossible to escape being pulled inside.

▲ Strong forces distort the star. If it passes too close it will be ripped apart.

160 Streams of matter shoot away from some black holes. Why this occurs precisely remains a mystery. The supermassive black hole at the centre of the M87 galaxy ejects a stream of hot gas that is an incredible 5000 light years in length.

▲ Matter from the star is drawn towards a black hole and can form a disc of material around the black hole called an accretion disc.

161 Some black holes spin fast. A black hole called GRS 1915+105 lies about 35,000 light years from Earth and is spinning around at incredible speed – between 950 and 1150 times every second.

▲ A black hole ejects a massive jet or stream of matter. This can measure many light years in length.

Families of stars

162 A galaxy is a giant collection of stars. These are all held together by gravity. Inside even the smallest galaxies are more than a million stars. The biggest galaxies hold many billions of stars. Galaxies also contain large clouds of gas, dust, planets and the remains of old stars.

▲ The two colliding Antennae galaxies (NGC 4038 and NGC 4039) create a spectacular sight. Within 400 million years, they will form a single galaxy.

163 The biggest known galaxy, IC1101, is 50 times wider than our Milky Way. It lies 1.07 billion light years away and is around six million light years wide. Scientists estimate that it may contain as many as 100 thousand billion stars.

164 Occasionally, two galaxies collide, forming lots of new stars. The Antennae galaxies started colliding a few hundred million years ago. As the two galaxies crash into each other, gas and dust is pressed together. The energy from the collision forms new stars.

▲ I Zwicky 18 galaxy was once thought to be very young. Further studies have discovered it has some faint stars that are as much as 10 billion years old.

165
Galaxies can vary greatly in age. When astronomers first spied I Zwicky 18, they thought it was a young galaxy because most of its stars were only 500 million years old. Galaxy UDFy-38135539 is thought to be over 13.2 billion years old, making it the oldest object scientists have observed in the Universe.

166
There are more than 170 billion galaxies in the Universe. That's 24 galaxies for every person on Earth! As telescopes and other scientific instruments used to look into space improve and reach further and deeper into space, astronomers may find even more.

▼ The Hubble Space Telescope's Deep Field and Ultra Deep Field observations peer back in time to incredibly distant and old galaxies formed relatively shortly after the Big Bang.

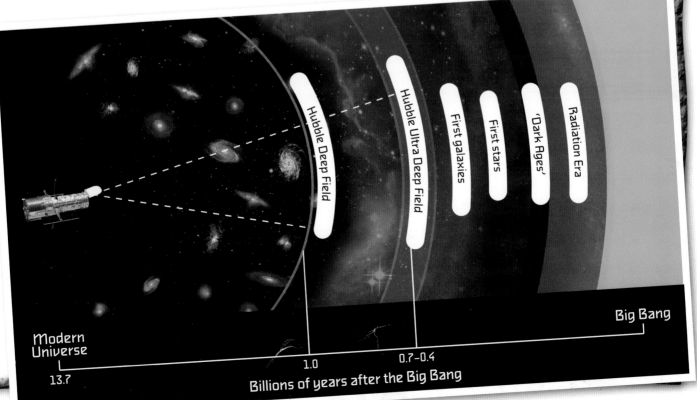

Modern Universe

Hubble Deep Field

Hubble Ultra Deep Field

First galaxies

First stars

'Dark Ages'

Radiation Era

Big Bang

13.7   1.0   0.7–0.4

Billions of years after the Big Bang

Types of galaxy

167 Astronomers group galaxies together according to their shape. Elliptical galaxies form round or oval shapes. They don't rotate much and don't contain many new stars. Spiral galaxies, such as our Milky Way and NGC 253 have plenty of gas and dust for new star formation.

▼ M87 is an elliptical galaxy at least 120,000 light years wide and containing over two trillion stars.

168 Some galaxies are dwarfs, a tiny fraction of the size of the Milky Way. Recent discoveries have shown that lots of little galaxies exist that are jam-packed with stars. These are called ultra compact dwarf galaxies.

▼ NGC 253 galaxy is one of the brightest spiral galaxies visible, and also one of the dustiest, which means lots of stars are formed at a rapid rate.

QUIZ
1. What type of galaxy is NGC 253?
2. Which galaxy contains the most stars: M87 or M60-UCD1?
3. By what name is NGC 6822 galaxy also known?

Answers:
1. Spiral galaxy 2. M87
3. Barnard's Galaxy

169 A newly discovered galaxy called M60-UCD1 is an ultra compact dwarf galaxy. It is just 160 light years wide, but home to as many as 140 million stars. Stars in this galaxy are packed at least 25 times closer than in our part of the Milky Way.

170 Irregular galaxies have no clear shape. Astronomers believe they formed due to a collision with another galaxy some time in the past. As a result, many irregular galaxies have a mix of baby protostars, young stars and old stars.

▲ NGC 6822, also known as Barnard's Galaxy, is an irregular dwarf galaxy about 1.6 million light years away. It contains around 10 million stars, young and old.

171 Around three quarters of all galaxies are spiral galaxies. They have long curved arms and turn around the galaxy's centre, or hub. The shape of the hub may be circular, or if it is more rectangular it is known as a barred spiral.

◄ A barred spiral galaxy has a large number of bright stars running across its centre.

Our home galaxy

172 Our Solar System is part of the huge Milky Way galaxy. Our home galaxy is a spiral around 100–120,000 light years wide. It's about 1000 light years thick except in the bulging centre called the hub, which is around 5–7 times thicker.

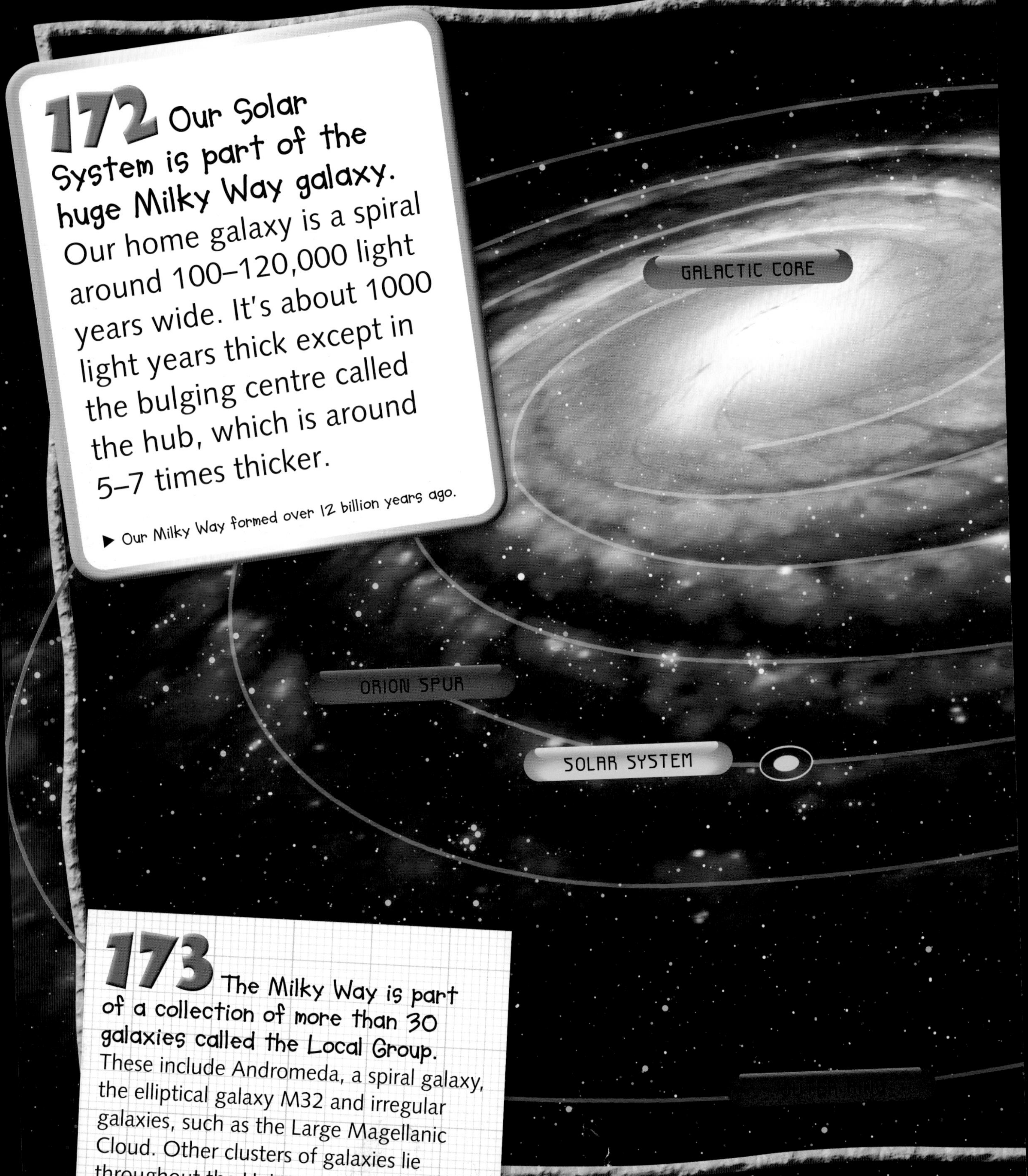

▶ Our Milky Way formed over 12 billion years ago.

GALACTIC CORE

ORION SPUR

SOLAR SYSTEM

173 The Milky Way is part of a collection of more than 30 galaxies called the Local Group. These include Andromeda, a spiral galaxy, the elliptical galaxy M32 and irregular galaxies, such as the Large Magellanic Cloud. Other clusters of galaxies lie throughout the Universe.

CRUX-SCRUTUM

SAGITTARIUS ARM

PERSEUS ARM

175 Like Earth orbits the Sun, our Solar System orbits the centre of the Milky Way. It does so at high speed – around 792,000 kilometres per hour or 220 kilometres every second. Even at this speed, a galactic year (which is the time it takes for the Solar System to complete its orbit) lasts over 225 million years.

174 The Sun is just one of more than 100 billion stars in the Milky Way. Many millions are contained in the central bulge and in the two largest spiral arms, the Perseus arm and the Sagittarius arm.

176 From face-on, astronomers believe the Milky Way looks like a giant Catherine wheel. From its hub, around 27,000 light years across, long spiral arms of stars and gas curve out from the centre.

Seeing stars

177 **Ancient astronomers used just their eyes to spot the stars.** Some ancient astronomers mapped the position and movement of stars in great detail. The Greek astronomer, Hipparchus, made an amazing catalogue of over 800 stars more than 2100 years ago. On a clear night a person can see around 2000 stars in the sky.

▲ Ancient Babylonian astronomers were among the first to produce catalogues of stars they observed, written on clay tablets over 3200 years ago.

178 **Many amateur telescopes have a 10 centimetre aperture.** However, the Gran Telescopio Canarias (GTC) scientific telescope is 100 times as big. A bigger aperture means that more light can be gathered. The GTC is the biggest reflecting telescope in the world. Its aperture measures 10.4 metres wide, enabling it to gather light from really distant galaxies.

▼ Located at an altitude of 2326 metres, the Gran Telescopio Canarias is the largest single optical telescope in the worlld.

179 **Optical telescopes magnify distant objects to bring them closer.** Optical telescopes gather more light than your eye can and focus it to a give a clearer, larger view of distant objects. The first telescopes were invented by Dutch spectacles makers who placed two lenses in a tube in 1608.

Integrated Science Instrument
Module (ISIM)

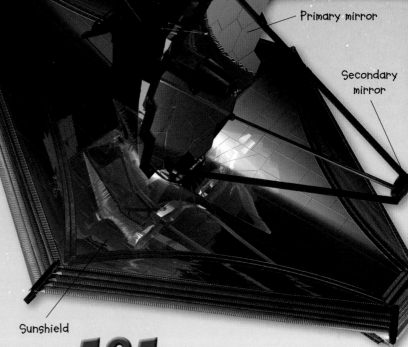

Primary mirror

Secondary
mirror

Sunshield

▶ The James Webb's large
6.4-metre-diameter mirror will give
the telescope around seven times more
light-gathering power than the Hubble.

180 Reflecting
telescopes use mirrors
instead of lenses. Invented
by British scientist, Sir Isaac
Newton in 1668, reflecting
telescopes focus light by bouncing
it off a series of mirrors. It is easier
to make big mirrors than big
lenses so the biggest optical
telescopes used today by
astronomers are reflectors.

181 The James Webb space
telescope will launch in 2018. It is twice
as big as the existing Hubble telescope and
will peer even deeper into space. It will look
for the oldest objects and galaxies formed
after the Big Bang, as well as signs of
life on exoplanets.

▼ Sir Isaac Newton's first
reflecting telescope used a
piece of polished tin-copper
metal alloy as a mirror.

I DON'T BELIEVE IT!
The Hubble Space Telescope has
taken over 700,000 photos of
stars, galaxies and
other things in space
since it was sent
into space in 1990.

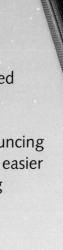

83

Patterns in the sky

182 Stars form patterns in the night sky. Different people in the past gave these patterns different names. In the 1920s, these were reorganized into 88 different named areas in the night sky, known as constellations. Some are named after characters in ancient myths, such as Hercules and Orion or after animals, such as Leo (lion) or Lupus (wolf).

KEY

1. Cassiopeia – mythical Queen
2. Ursa Major – Great Bear
3. Draco – dragon
4. Cygnus – swan
5. Hydra – water snake

183 Not all stars can be seen at one time. As Earth travels on its orbit around the Sun, different stars can be seen at different times of the year. This is why maps of the night sky differ depending on the months or seasons of the year.

▶ This diagram shows how our line of sight alters depending on Earth's movement around the Sun.

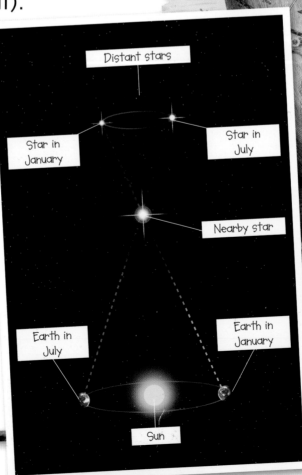

Distant stars

Star in January

Star in July

Nearby star

Earth in July

Earth in January

Sun

▲ This 17th century map of the constellations shows how many were named after mythical people, gods or creatures.

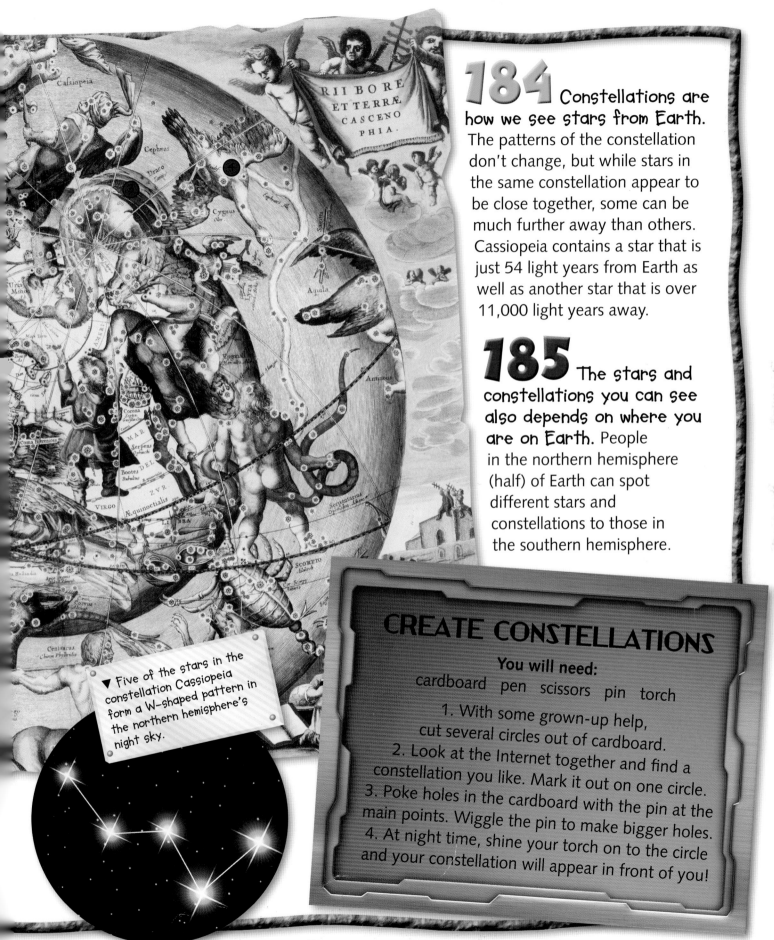

184 Constellations are how we see stars from Earth. The patterns of the constellation don't change, but while stars in the same constellation appear to be close together, some can be much further away than others. Cassiopeia contains a star that is just 54 light years from Earth as well as another star that is over 11,000 light years away.

185 The stars and constellations you can see also depends on where you are on Earth. People in the northern hemisphere (half) of Earth can spot different stars and constellations to those in the southern hemisphere.

▼ Five of the stars in the constellation Cassiopeia form a W-shaped pattern in the northern hemisphere's night sky.

CREATE CONSTELLATIONS

You will need:
cardboard   pen   scissors   pin   torch

1. With some grown-up help, cut several circles out of cardboard.
2. Look at the Internet together and find a constellation you like. Mark it out on one circle.
3. Poke holes in the cardboard with the pin at the main points. Wiggle the pin to make bigger holes.
4. At night time, shine your torch on to the circle and your constellation will appear in front of you!

Capturing waves

186 Stars and galaxies don't just give off light. Visible light, which travels in waves, is just one form of electromagnetic radiation. Other types exist, such as ultraviolet, which is mostly emitted by young stars and white dwarfs. Instruments capture these waves and tell us more about objects in space.

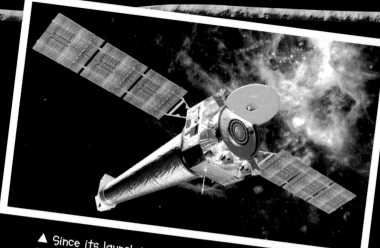

▲ Since its launch in 1999, the Chandra X-ray Observatory has made many discoveries, including finding neutron stars, black holes and young stars bursting into life.

187 When stars collide or explode as a supernova, they give off bursts of radiation called gamma rays. Gamma rays can contain huge amounts of energy. A major gamma ray burst can release more energy in ten seconds than the Sun will give off in its lifetime.

▶ Fermi is a scientific satellite, which carries a telescope to scan the Universe for gamma rays.

188 X-rays are given off by stars and other objects hotter than 1 million°C. Neutron stars, hot gas close to black holes and supernovae remnants all give off X-rays, which can be detected by special telescopes, such as the Chandra Observatory.

▶ These two images show the same spiral galaxy using two methods. The top one is a black and white image using visible light only. The bottom one is an X-ray image.

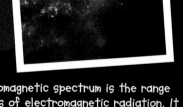

▼ The electromagnetic spectrum is the range of frequencies of electromagnetic radiation. It ranges from the high frequencies of gamma rays to the low frequency of radio communication.

Electromagnetic energy

| Gamma ray | X-ray | Ultraviolet |

189

Infrared is a type of radiation that can travel through clouds of dust and gas. The Infrared Astronomical Satellite (IRAS) discovered over 300,000 sources of infrared waves from space. Thousands of these were starburst galaxies with new stars forming inside them.

I DON'T BELIEVE IT!
The biggest single radio telescope dish has a diameter of 305 metres – as long as three soccer pitches.

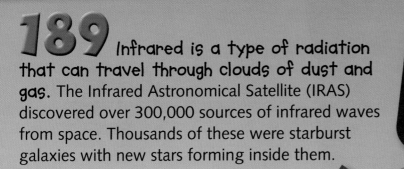

▼ This infrared image of the Andromeda Galaxy was taken by IRAS and is red and orange where the strongest infrared waves are given out, and blue where the weakest are emitted.

▲ The Spitzer space telescope collects infrared waves given off by cooler objects, such as brown dwarf stars and dust at the centre of galaxies.

190

Many objects in space were discovered using radio telescopes. These huge dishes, sometimes as big as 300 metres in diameter, gather signals from large clouds of gas, dust and pulsars. A series of radio telescope dishes working together is called an array.

▼ The ALMA telescope array in Chile features 66 dishes, which can work together. Fifty of these dishes are 12 metres in diameter and weigh 85–115 tonnes each.

| Visible | Infrared | Microwave | Radio |

New worlds

191 Planets outside the Solar System are called exoplanets. More than 1800 of these have been discovered, since the first one was confirmed in 1992. Planets form from the disc of dust and gas that often swirls around a new star. This could mean many stars have planets orbiting them.

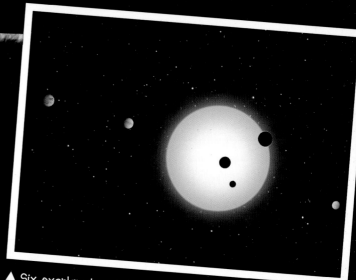

▲ Six exoplanets orbit around the Kepler-11 star. Its closet planet, Kepler b, is just one tenth of the distance that Earth is from the Sun.

◀ Kepler orbits the Sun and seeks out stars with planets orbiting them. It has already helped discover over 1000 exoplanets.

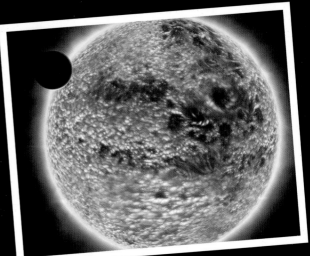

▲ The exoplanet HD 189733 b is a little bigger than Jupiter, but orbits its star in just 2.2 days.

192 One exoplanet's atmosphere possibly rains glass, not water. The conditions on HD 189733 b exoplanet are very hostile, with extreme temperatures and high winds. The atmosphere contains particles of silica – the material from which glass is made.

▲ The habitable zones are shown in green around three different types of star (from top): a hot star, a Sun-like star and a cooler star.

193 **The solar system is just one star system.** Five planets are known to orbit the Kepler 186, a star with around half the mass of the Sun. At least seven planets have been found in the Gliese 667c star system.

194 **Scientists are excited by finding exoplanets in the 'goldilocks zone' or habitable zone.** This is where exoplanets, like Gliese 667Cc, orbit within an area that is close enough to their star to be the right temperature for life to form. Exoplanets in the goldilocks zone may have water and the other things life needs to exist.

195 **Exoplanets can take hours to travel around their star or thousands of years.** Exoplanet Fomalhaut b, is believed to take around 2000 years to complete an orbit of its star. WASP-12b exoplanet only takes 26 hours to complete its journey around its star.

▼ This illustration shows a possible exoplanet, orbiting the Gliese 581 star, which is around 20 light years from Earth.

196 No extraterrestrials or aliens have been found... yet. Many scientists believe that the Universe is so vast that life must exist elsewhere. Our knowledge of the Universe is constantly changing with new discoveries being made every year.

▲ Kepler 186f is about 10 percent bigger than Earth, and takes 129.9 days to complete an orbit around its star.

197 Only one human-made object has ever left the Solar System. The *Voyager 1* space probe was launched in 1977 and left the Solar System in 2014. Although it is racing along at a rate of 1.5 million kilometres per day, it will still take thousands of years to reach another star system.

198 Exoplanet Kepler 186f was discovered in 2014. Scientists are excited because it is approximately the same size as Earth, and the right distance away from its star to potentially support life.

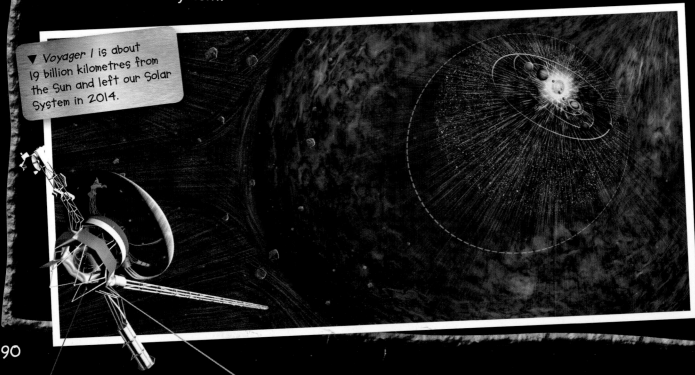

▼ Voyager I is about 19 billion kilometres from the Sun and left our Solar System in 2014.

199
Alien life might be quite different to Earth. Some planets have heavier atmospheres, which would support enormous flying creatures, for example, while on other planets living things might not even need water or oxygen to survive outer space.

▶ Tardigrades (one millimetre in size) are the first animals to survive exposure in space, surviving sub-zero temperatures, solar radiation and no oxygen.

200
Scientists have sent many welcome messages into space. Four space probes (*Pioneer 10* and *11*, and *Voyager 1* and *2*) carry gold plaques or discs showing pictures of humans and our place in the Solar System. Radio telescopes, such as the giant Arecibo dish in Puerto Rico, have also beamed messages into space. Earth is still waiting for a reply.

▲ Pioneer 11 was launched in 1973. It was built to last 21 months, but kept sending information back to Earth until 1995.

▲ Voyager's gold disc contained technical images showing how to play its record on the other side, as well as Earth's location from 14 stars.

I DON'T BELIEVE IT!
The gold discs carried by *Voyager 1* and *2* could also be played to reveal sounds of Earth as well as greetings in 55 different languages.

ASTRONOMY

201 Astronomy is the study of everything you can see in the night sky and many other things out in space. Astronomers try to find out all about stars and galaxies. They look for planets circling around stars, and at mysterious explosions far out in space. Telescopes help them to see further, spotting things that are much too faint to see with just their eyes.

▼ New stars are forming in this cloud of dark dust and glowing gas in space. It is called the Pelican Nebula.

Shining stars

202 Stars are huge balls of hot gas. They look tiny to us because they are so far away. Deep in the centre of a star it is so hot that some of the gas turns into energy. Stars shine by sending out this energy as light and heat.

203 A star starts life in a cloud of dust and gas called a nebula. Thicker parts of the cloud collapse into a ball that becomes a star. Sometimes a star will shine until its gas is used up, and then swell into a red giant star. A large star may then explode as a supernova but smaller ones just shrink, becoming tiny white dwarf stars.

204 A star's colour shows how hot it is. Red stars are small and cool, yellow ones are bigger and hotter, and white ones are huge and very hot. Dying stars get even bigger, becoming giants or supergiants.

▶ The Milky Way Galaxy looks like a band of light, instead of a spiral shape, because we are looking through it from inside one of the spiral arms.

BUTTERFLY NEBULA

At the end of its life a red giant star threw out this glowing cloud of gas.

STAR CLUSTER

The Quintuplet cluster is a group of bright young stars. They shine with different colours – red, blue and white.

M81 GALAXY

This huge spiral galaxy contains billions of stars. Our Milky Way Galaxy would look like this if we could see it from above.

I DON'T BELIEVE IT!
After it explodes as a supernova, a giant star may collapse, forming a black hole. The gravity of a black hole is so strong that it pulls everything into it — not even light can escape!

205 Galaxies are huge families of stars. Some are shaped like squashed balls, and these are called elliptical galaxies. Others have a spiral shape with arms curling out from a central ball of stars. Our Sun is in a spiral galaxy called the Milky Way. On very clear, dark nights you can see it as a faint band of light across the sky.

206 Using powerful telescopes, astronomers can see galaxies in all directions. They think there are many billions of galaxies, each containing billions of stars. All these stars and galaxies are part of the Universe. This is the name we give to everything we know about, including all the galaxies, our Sun and Moon, the Earth and everything on it, including you.

Our place in space

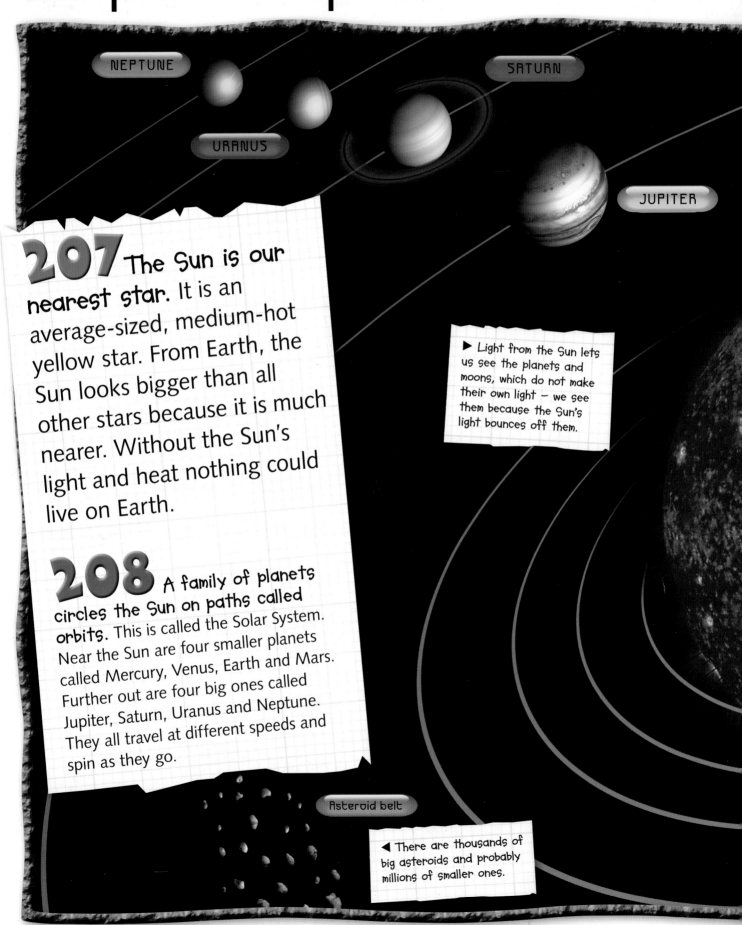

NEPTUNE

URANUS

SATURN

JUPITER

207 The Sun is our nearest star. It is an average-sized, medium-hot yellow star. From Earth, the Sun looks bigger than all other stars because it is much nearer. Without the Sun's light and heat nothing could live on Earth.

► Light from the Sun lets us see the planets and moons, which do not make their own light — we see them because the Sun's light bounces off them.

208 A family of planets circles the Sun on paths called orbits. This is called the Solar System. Near the Sun are four smaller planets called Mercury, Venus, Earth and Mars. Further out are four big ones called Jupiter, Saturn, Uranus and Neptune. They all travel at different speeds and spin as they go.

Asteroid belt

◄ There are thousands of big asteroids and probably millions of smaller ones.

209 All the planets except Mercury and Venus have moons circling them. Mars has two tiny ones. Earth has one large Moon – a round rocky ball with no air. The giant planets all have large families of moons – Jupiter and Saturn have over 60 each. Some of these are large, like our Moon, but most are small and icy.

SUN

Earth's moon

EARTH

VENUS

MERCURY

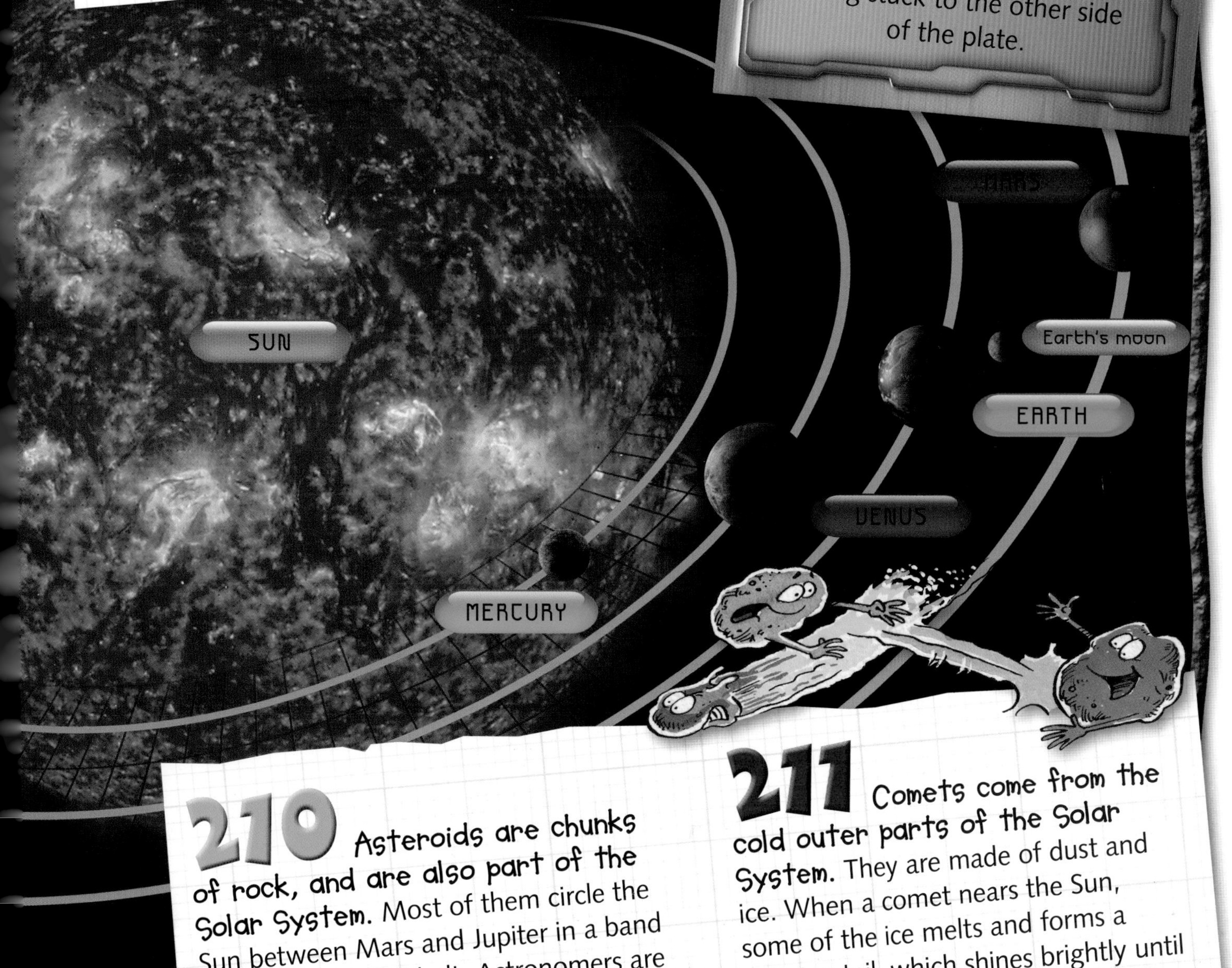

210 Asteroids are chunks of rock, and are also part of the Solar System. Most of them circle the Sun between Mars and Jupiter in a band called the asteroid belt. Astronomers are always on the lookout for asteroids that might hit the Earth.

211 Comets come from the cold outer parts of the Solar System. They are made of dust and ice. When a comet nears the Sun, some of the ice melts and forms a glowing tail, which shines brightly until it moves away again.

Planets large and small

212 Mercury is the smallest planet and closest to the Sun. This rocky ball is very hot during the day, but freezing at night because it has no air to hold heat. Venus is about the same size as Earth. It is covered with clouds that trap heat so it is even hotter than Mercury.

EARTH
Length of day: 24 hours
Length of year: 365 days
Special features: Earth is the only planet where life is known to exist

MARS
Length of day: 24.6 Earth hours
Length of year: 687 Earth days
Special features: The largest volcano in the Solar System, called Olympus Mons

► Mars has ice caps in the far north and south, like the Arctic and Antarctic on Earth.

MERCURY
Length of day: 59 Earth days
Length of year: 88 Earth days
Special features: Many craters made by space rocks crashing into the planet billions of years ago

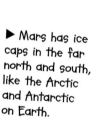

VENUS
Length of day: 243 Earth days
Length of year: 225 Earth days
Special features: Thick atmosphere pressing down so hard it would crush any visiting astronaut

▼ Venus has volcanoes all over its surface. This one, called Maat Mons, is the tallest.

213 The planet we live on – Earth – is the third planet from the Sun. It is mostly covered with water and it has air, both of which living things need to survive, so all kinds of animals and plants can thrive here. Mars is the furthest of the small rocky planets from the Sun. Its dry surface is covered with reddish dust and rocks.

JUPITER

Length of day: 9.9 Earth hours
Length of year: 11.86 Earth years
Special features: The Great Red Spot, a giant storm that is larger than Earth

SATURN

Length of day: 10.7 Earth hours
Length of year: 29.46 Earth years
Special features: Bright rings made of chunks of ice that speed round it

▶ Colours have been added to this picture of Saturn to show its many separate rings.

214 Jupiter and Saturn are giants of the Solar System. Neither has a solid surface – they are made of mainly gas and liquid. Jupiter is the largest planet. It has stripy clouds and a huge storm called the Great Red Spot. Saturn is surrounded by rings made of icy chunks that orbit it.

215 Uranus and Neptune are furthest from the Sun. They are icy cold because they get so little heat from the Sun. Both are completely covered with deep clouds.

216 A growing number of dwarf planets, smaller than the main planets, are being discovered. Pluto is a dwarf planet although it was originally the ninth planet. Ceres, which was called the largest asteroid, is another. The other three – Haumea, Makemake and Eris – are recent discoveries, and are so far away that we know very little about them.

URANUS

Length of day: 17.24 Earth hours
Length of year: 84 Earth years
Special features: Does not spin upright so it looks like it is rolling round the Sun

NEPTUNE

Length of day: 16.1 Earth hours
Length of year: 165 Earth years
Special features: The strongest winds in the Solar System blow icy clouds round the planet

▶ White clouds float above dark storms that come and go on Neptune's blue cloudy surface.

I DON'T BELIEVE IT!

The Earth is speeding round the Sun at 29.8 kilometres a second – more than 100,000 kilometres an hour. That's about 100 times faster than a jet airliner!

Starry skies

217 People have always been fascinated by the stars and Moon. Ancient people watched the Sun cross the sky during the day and disappear at night. Then when it got dark they saw the Moon and stars move across the sky. They wondered what caused these things to happen.

218 Sometimes the Sun goes dark in the middle of the day. This is called a solar eclipse, and it is caused by the Moon moving in front of the Sun, blocking its light. People in the past did not know this, so eclipses were scary. In ancient China, people thought they were caused by a dragon eating the Sun.

219 In ancient times people did not know what the Sun, Moon and stars were. Many thought the Sun was a god. The ancient Egyptians called this god Ra. They believed he rode across the sky in a boat each day and was swallowed by the sky goddess, Nut, every evening and then born again the next morning.

▲ The Egyptians pictured their sky goddess Nut with a starry body and their sun god Ra sitting on a throne.

◀ Ancient Chinese people fired arrows and banged pots and pans during eclipses, believing this would frighten the dragon away.

▲ The Bayeux Tapestry, made during the 1070s, shows people pointing at the famous Halley's comet (at the top right).

◀ The Greek sun god, Helios, rode across the sky in a chariot pulled by four horses.

220 Early astronomers could not predict when comets would appear. Comets were known as 'long-haired stars' because of their glowing tails, and many people thought they brought bad luck. They were blamed for disasters, from floods and famines to defeat in battle.

▶ Quetzalcoatl was a feathered serpent, and to the Aztec people of Central America he was the god of the morning star.

Mapping the stars

221 Ancient astronomers made maps of star patterns, dividing them into groups called constellations. People around the world all grouped the stars differently. Today, astronomers recognize 88 constellations that cover the whole sky.

▼ Old star maps showed the constellations as animals such as Draco the Dragon and Ursa Minor the Little Bear.

▼ The northern half of the Earth has different constellations from the southern half, but all the star patterns stay the same night after night.

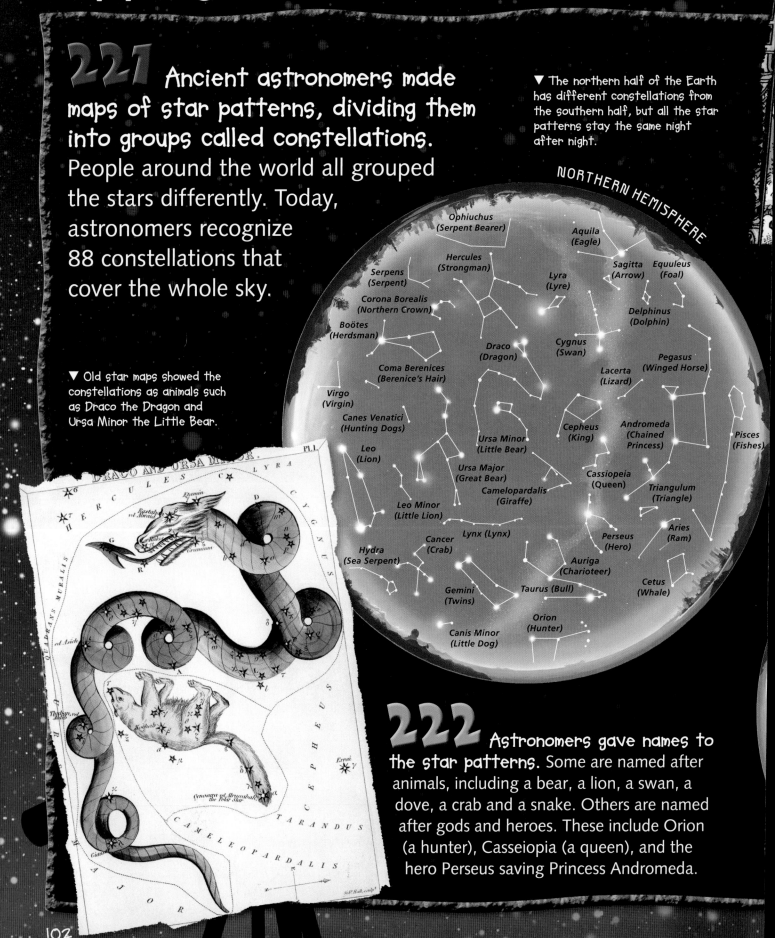

NORTHERN HEMISPHERE

Ophiuchus (Serpent Bearer)
Aquila (Eagle)
Hercules (Strongman)
Sagitta (Arrow)
Equuleus (Foal)
Serpens (Serpent)
Lyra (Lyre)
Corona Borealis (Northern Crown)
Delphinus (Dolphin)
Boötes (Herdsman)
Draco (Dragon)
Cygnus (Swan)
Pegasus (Winged Horse)
Coma Berenices (Berenice's Hair)
Lacerta (Lizard)
Virgo (Virgin)
Canes Venatici (Hunting Dogs)
Cepheus (King)
Andromeda (Chained Princess)
Pisces (Fishes)
Leo (Lion)
Ursa Minor (Little Bear)
Ursa Major (Great Bear)
Cassiopeia (Queen)
Triangulum (Triangle)
Camelopardalis (Giraffe)
Leo Minor (Little Lion)
Aries (Ram)
Lynx (Lynx)
Perseus (Hero)
Cancer (Crab)
Hydra (Sea Serpent)
Auriga (Charioteer)
Cetus (Whale)
Gemini (Twins)
Taurus (Bull)
Orion (Hunter)
Canis Minor (Little Dog)

222 Astronomers gave names to the star patterns. Some are named after animals, including a bear, a lion, a swan, a dove, a crab and a snake. Others are named after gods and heroes. These include Orion (a hunter), Casseiopia (a queen), and the hero Perseus saving Princess Andromeda.

◄ Here an ancient astronomer (bottom left) is pictured comically looking through the starry celestial sphere to see how it moves.

224
Stars appear to move across the sky at night. This is because the Earth is spinning all the time, but in the past people thought the stars were fixed to the inside of a huge hollow ball called the celestial sphere, which moved slowly around the Earth.

223
Over 2000 years ago, the Greek astronomer Hipparchus made a catalogue of over 850 stars. He listed their brightness and positions, and called the brightest ones first magnitude stars. Astronomers still call the brightness of a star its magnitude.

SPOT A STAR PATTERN
You will need:
clear night   warm clothes   dark place   good view of the sky
If you live in the North, look for the saucepan-shape of the Big Dipper – four stars for the bowl and three for the handle. If you live in the South, look overhead for four stars in the shape of a cross – the Southern Cross.

225
Ancient astronomers noticed that one star seems to stay still while the others circle around it. This is the Pole Star. It is above the North Pole and shows which direction is north. The ancient Egyptians used this knowledge to align the sides of the pyramids exactly.

SOUTHERN HEMISPHERE

Lepus (Hare), Canis Major (Great Dog), Columba (Dove), Eridanus (River Eridanus), Sextans (Sextant), Puppis (Stern), Carina (Keel) and Vela (Sail), Caelum (Chisel), Pictor (Painter's Easel), Fornax (Furnace), Hydra (Sea Serpent), Reticulum (Net), Dorado (Goldfish), Phoenix (Phoenix), Cetus (Whale), Volans (Flying Fish), Crater (Cup), Crux (Southern Cross), Chamaeleon (Chameleon), Grus (Crane), Tucana (Toucan), and Pavo (Peacock), Corvus (Crow), Centaurus (Centaur), Musca (Fly), Apus (Bird of Paradise), Virgo (Virgin), Triangulum Australe (Southern Triangle), Indus (Indian), Aquarius (Water Carrier), Ara (Altar), Piscis Austrinus (Southern Fish), Scorpius (Scorpion), Corona Australis (Southern Crown), Libra (Scales), Capricornus (Sea Goat), Serpens (Serpent) and Ophiuchus (Serpent Bearer), Sagittarius (Archer)

Keeping time

226 The Sun, Moon and stars can be used to measure time. It takes a day for the Earth to spin round, and a year for it to circle the Sun. By observing changes in the positions of constellations, astronomers worked out the length of a year so they could make a calendar.

227 It takes 29.5 days for the Moon to circle the Earth. The Moon seems to change shape because we see different amounts of its sunlit side as it goes round the Earth. When the sunlit side faces Earth we see a Full Moon. When it faces away, we see only a thin crescent shape.

Day 1
Day 3 Crescent Moon
Day 5
Day 7 Half Moon
Day 10
Day 14 Full Moon
Day 17
Day 19
Day 21 Half Moon
Day 24
Day 26 Crescent Moon
Day 28 New Moon

▲ The Moon's changing shapes are called the phases of the Moon. It doesn't really change shape — it is always a round ball of rock.

228 Ancient people used sundials to tell the time.

A sundial consists of an upright rod and a flat plate. When the Sun shines, the rod casts a shadow on the plate. As the Sun moves across the sky, the shadow moves round the plate. Marks on the plate indicate the hours.

229 As the Earth circles the Sun, different stars appear in the sky.

This helped people predict when seasons would change. In ancient Egypt the bright star Sirius showed when the river Nile would flood, making the land ready for crops.

MAKE A SUNDIAL

You will need:
short stick   plasticine   card
pencil   clock

1. Stand the stick upright on the card using the plasticine. Put it outside on a sunny day.
2. Every hour, make a pencil mark on the card where the shadow ends.
3. Leave the card where it is and the shadow will point to the time whenever the Sun is out.

▼ The shadow made by this sundial points to the time, which is marked on the round dial.

◄ Stonehenge's huge upright stones are lined up with sunrise on the longest day in midsummer and on the shortest day in midwinter.

230 Stonehenge is an ancient monument in England that is lined up with the Sun and Moon.

It is a circle of giant stones over 4000 years old. It may have been used as a calendar, or an observatory to predict when eclipses would happen.

Wandering stars

231 When people began to study the stars they spotted five that were unlike the rest. Instead of staying in fixed patterns, they moved across the constellations, and they did not twinkle. Astronomers called them planets, which means 'wandering stars'.

232 The planets are named after ancient Roman gods. Mercury is the messenger of the gods, Venus is the god of love, Mars is the god of war, Jupiter is king of the gods and Saturn is the god of farming. Later astronomers used telescopes to find two more planets, and named them Uranus and Neptune after the gods of the sky and the sea.

233 At first people thought that the Earth was at the centre of everything. They believed the Sun, Moon and planets all circled the Earth. The ancient Greek astronomer Ptolemy thought the Moon was nearest Earth, then Mercury and Venus, then the Sun, and finally Jupiter and Saturn.

▼ Ptolemy's picture of the Solar System shows the Earth in the middle and the Sun and planets moving round it in circles.

DRAW AN ELLIPSE

You will need:
two drawing pins   paper
thick card   pencil   string

1. Place the paper on the card. Push the pins into the paper, placing them a little way apart.
2. Tie the string into a loop that fits loosely round the pins.
3. Using the pencil point, pull the string tight into a triangle shape.
4. Move the pencil round on the paper, keeping the string tight to draw an ellipse.

234

Astronomers measured the positions and movements of the planets. What they found did not fit Ptolemy's ideas. In 1543, the Polish astronomer Nicolaus Copernicus suggested that the planets circled the Sun. This explained much of what the astronomers saw, but still didn't fit the measurements exactly.

◄ Nicolaus Copernicus' view placed the Sun in the middle with the Earth moving round it with the other planets.

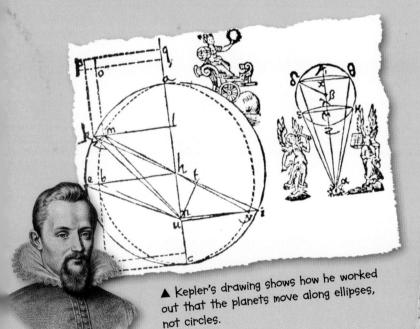

▲ Kepler's drawing shows how he worked out that the planets move along ellipses, not circles.

235

German astronomer Johannes Kepler published his solution to this problem in 1609. He realized that the orbits of Earth and the planets were not perfect circles, but ellipses (slightly squashed circles). This fitted all the measurements and describes the Solar System as we know it today.

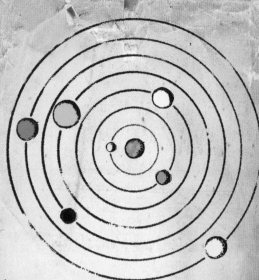

① From above, Ptolemy's plan shows everything (from inside to outside: Earth's Moon, Mercury, Venus, Sun, Mars, Jupiter, Saturn) moving round the Earth.

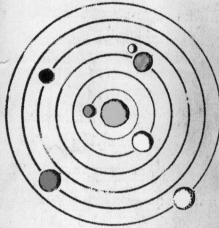

② Copernicus' view changes this to show everything moving round the Sun.

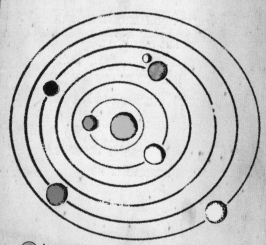

③ Kepler changes the circular paths of the planets into ellipses.

First telescopes

236 The telescope was invented in about 1608. Telescopes use two lenses (discs of glass that bulge out in the middle, or curve inwards) – one at each end of a tube. When you look through a telescope, distant things look nearer and larger.

237 Italian scientist Galileo built a telescope in 1609. He was one of the first people to use the new invention for astronomy. With it, Galileo observed craters and mountains on the Moon, and discovered four moons circling the planet Jupiter. He was also amazed to see many more stars in the sky.

▲ Galileo shows a crowd of people the exciting new things he can see through his telescope.

Mirror

JUPITER

IO

EUROPA

CALLISTO

GANYMEDE

▲ Jupiter's four largest moons are called the Galilean moons, because Galileo was the first person to see them using his telescope.

238 When Galileo looked at the planet Venus through his telescope he saw that it sometimes appeared to be crescent shaped, just like the Moon. This meant that Venus was circling the Sun and not the Earth and helped to prove that Copernicus was right about the planets circling the Sun. Galileo described his amazing discoveries in a book called *The Starry Messenger*.

239 Other astronomers were soon trying to build more powerful telescopes. In 1668, English scientist Isaac Newton made one in which he replaced one of the lenses with a curved mirror, shaped like a saucer. He had invented the reflecting telescope. Large modern telescopes are based on Newton's invention.

Eyepiece

Sliding focus

Ball mounting

I DON'T BELIEVE IT!
According to legend, Newton began to think about gravity when he saw an apple fall from a tree, and wondered why the apple fell to the ground instead of floating up.

240 Newton also worked out why the planets orbit the Sun. He realized that something was pulling the planets towards the Sun – a pulling force called gravity. The pull of the Sun's gravity keeps the planets in their orbits, and the Earth's gravity holds the Moon in its orbit. It also prevents everything on Earth from floating off into space.

◀ The mirror in Newton's telescope gave a clearer image of the stars than telescopes with lenses.

Discoveries with telescopes

▶ Halley's comet was last seen in 1986 and will return again in 2061.

241 Astronomers made many new discoveries with their telescopes. The English astronomer Edmund Halley was interested in comets. He thought that a bright comet seen in 1682 was the same as one that was seen in 1607, and predicted that it would return in 1758. His prediction was right and the comet was named after him – Halley's Comet.

◀ Halley also mapped the stars and studied the Sun and Moon.

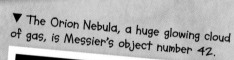
▼ The Orion Nebula, a huge glowing cloud of gas, is Messier's object number 42.

242 The French astronomer Charles Messier was also a comet hunter. In 1781 he tried to make his search easier by listing over 100 fuzzy objects in the sky that could be mistaken for comets. Later astronomers realized that some of these are glowing clouds of dust and gas and others are distant galaxies.

▲ Messier's object number 16 is the Eagle Nebula, a dusty cloud where stars are born.

▼ Messier's object number 31 is a giant spiral galaxy called Andromeda.

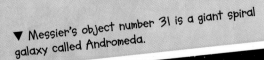

243 William Herschel, a German astronomer living in England, discovered a new planet in 1781. Using a reflecting telescope he had built himself, he spotted a star that seemed to move. It didn't look like a comet, and Herschel realized that it must be a new planet. It was the first planet discovered with a telescope and was called Uranus.

▲ William Herschel worked as astronomer for King George III of England.

244 Astronomers soon discovered that Uranus was not following its expected orbit. They thought another planet might be pulling it off course. Following predictions made by mathematicians, astronomers found another planet in 1846. It was called Neptune. It is so far away that it looks like a star.

245 The discovery of Neptune didn't fully explain Uranus' orbit. In 1930 an American astronomer, Clyde Tombaugh, found Pluto. It was the ninth planet from the Sun and much smaller than expected. In 2006 astronomers decided to call Pluto a dwarf planet.

▲ Herschel's great telescope was the largest telescope in the world at the time and its mirror measured 1.2 metres across.

QUIZ
1. Who discovered the planet Uranus?
2. When was Halley's Comet last seen?
3. Which was the ninth planet from the Sun until 2006?

Answers:
1. William Herschel 2. 1986 3. Pluto

How telescopes work

246 Telescopes make distant things look nearer. Most stars are so far away that even with a telescope they just look like points of light. But the Moon and planets seem much larger through a telescope – you can see details such as craters on the Moon and cloud patterns on Jupiter.

247 A reflecting telescope uses a curved mirror to collect light. The mirror reflects and focuses the light. A second, smaller mirror sends the light out through the side of the telescope or back through a hole in the big mirror to an eyepiece lens. Looking through the eyepiece lens you see a larger image of the distant object.

▶ Star light bounces off the main mirror of a reflecting telescope back up to the eyepiece lens near the top.

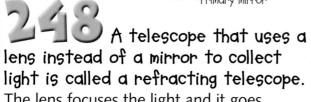

Eyepiece lens

Reflected light

Light enters

Secondary mirror

Primary mirror

248 A telescope that uses a lens instead of a mirror to collect light is called a refracting telescope. The lens focuses the light and it goes straight down the telescope tube to the eyepiece lens at the other end. Refracting telescopes are not as large as reflecting ones because large lenses are very heavy.

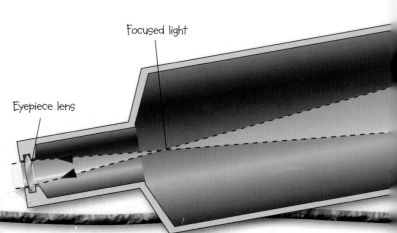

Focused light

Eyepiece lens

249 Astronomers are building telescopes with larger and larger mirrors. Bigger mirrors reveal fainter objects so telescopes can see further and further into the Universe. They also show more details in the distant galaxies and the wispy glowing clouds between the stars.

250 Today, professional astronomers don't look through their telescopes. They use cameras to capture the images. A camera can build up an image over a long time. The light adds up to make a brighter image, showing things that could not be seen by just looking through the telescope.

▲ A telescope reveals round craters on the Moon and large dark patches called 'seas' although the Moon is completely dry.

▲ The mirror from the Rosse Telescope in Ireland is 1.8 metres across and is kept in the Science Museum in London. One hundred years ago it was the largest telescope in the world.

▼ In a refracting telescope the main lens at the top bends the light, making an image near the bottom of the telescope.

Primary lens

Light enters

I DON'T BELIEVE IT!
The Liverpool telescope on the island of La Palma in the Atlantic Ocean is able to automatically observe a list of objects sent to it via the Internet.

Telescopes today

251 All large modern telescopes are reflecting telescopes. To make clear images, their mirrors must be exactly the right shape. The mirrors are made of polished glass, covered with a thin layer of aluminium to reflect as much light as possible. Some are made of thin glass that would sag without supports beneath to hold it in exactly the right shape.

252 Large telescope mirrors are often made up of many smaller mirrors. The mirrors of the Keck telescopes in Hawaii are made of 36 separate parts. Each has six sides, which fit together to make a mirror 10 metres across – about the width of a tennis court. The small mirrors are tilted to make exactly the right shape.

253 The air above a telescope is constantly moving. This can make their images blurred. Astronomers reduce this by using an extra mirror that can change shape. A computer works out what shape this mirror needs to be to remove the blurring effect and keeps changing it every few seconds. This is called adaptive optics.

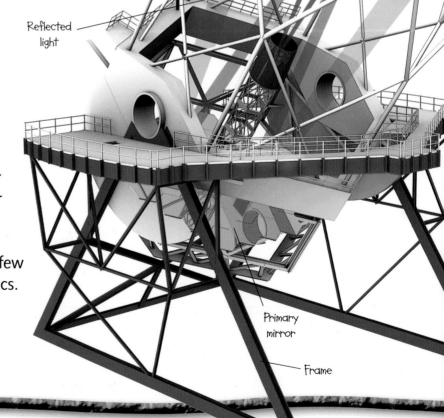

▶ A huge frame holds the mirrors of a large reflecting telescope in position while tilting and turning to point at the stars.

Light enters

Secondary mirror

Reflected light

Primary mirror

Frame

▲ The main mirror of the Gran Telescopio Canarias telescope measures 10.4 metres across when all its 36 separate parts are fitted together.

255 Large telescopes can work together to see finer detail than a single telescope. When the two Keck telescopes are linked, they produce images that are almost as good as a telescope with a mirror as wide as the distance between them – 85 metres, (about the length of a football field).

254 Telescopes must be able to move to track the stars. It may take hours to make an image of a very faint, distant target and during this time the target will move gradually across the sky. Motors drive the telescope at just the right speed to keep it pointing at the target. All the time the image is being recorded using CCDs like those in an ordinary digital camera.

QUIZ

1. What are telescope mirrors made of?
2. How many sides does each piece of a Keck telescope mirror have?
3. Why do telescopes have to move?

Answers:
1. Glass 2. 6
3. To track the stars

▶ This picture of Saturn was taken by one of the Keck telescopes. The orange colours have been added to show the different temperatures in its clouds and rings.

Observatories

256 **Observatories are places for watching the skies, often where telescopes are built and housed.** There are usually several telescopes of different sizes at the same observatory. Astronomers choose remote places far away from cities, as bright lights would spoil their observations.

257 **Observatories are often on the tops of mountains and in dry desert areas.** This is because the air close to the ground is constantly moving and full of clouds and dust. Astronomers need very clear, dry, still air so they build their telescopes as high as possible above most of the clouds and dust.

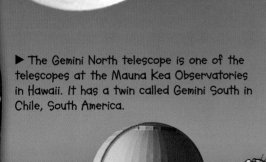

▶ The Gemini North telescope is one of the telescopes at the Mauna Kea Observatories in Hawaii. It has a twin called Gemini South in Chile, South America.

▲ The Very Large Telescope is really four large telescopes and four smaller ones. The large telescopes are inside the square domes.

258
A desert is a good place to build an observatory. The high mountains in the Atacama Desert, in Chile, South America, are among the driest places on Earth, and night skies there are incredibly dark. Several large telescopes have been built there including the Very Large Telescope (VLT).

259
Some famous observatories are on top of a dormant volcano called Mauna Kea, on the island of Hawaii. It is the highest mountain on an island in the world – most clouds are below it. It is a good place for astronomy because the air is very clean and dry. It has more clear nights than most other places on Earth. It has 13 telescopes, four of them very large.

Telescope inside

Raised shutter

Rotating dome

Building linking telescopes

▲ The two Keck telescopes at the Mauna Kea Observatories each have their own round dome with shutters that open to let in the starlight.

The Keck telescopes

▼ Observatories on Mauna Kea, Hawaii.

260
Domes cover the telescopes to protect them and keep the mirrors clean. The domes have shutters that open when the telescopes are operating to let in the starlight. They also turn round so that the telescope can point in any direction and can move to track the stars.

Splitting light

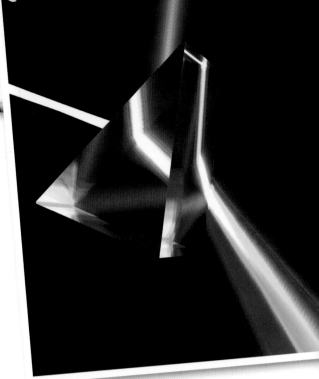

261 Astronomers find out about distant stars by studying the starlight that reaches Earth. They can get more data from the light by splitting it into its different colours – like a rainbow that forms when rain drops split up sunlight. These colours are called a spectrum.

▲ White light going in one side of a wedge-shaped glass prism spreads out into a rainbow of colours, making a spectrum.

RAINBOW SPECTRUM

You will need:
drinking glass   small mirror
water   torch   card

1. Put the mirror in the glass so that it faces upwards.
2. Pour water into the glass to cover the mirror.
3. In a dark room, shine the torch onto the mirror.
4. Hold the card to catch the reflected light from the mirror and see a rainbow – the water and mirror have split the light into a spectrum.

262 Astronomers can tell how hot a star is from its spectrum. The hottest are blue-white, the coolest are red, and in between are yellow and orange stars. The spectrum also shows how big and bright the star is so astronomers can tell which are ordinary stars and which are red giants or supergiants.

263 A star's spectrum can show what gases the star is made of. Each gas has a different pattern of lines in the spectrum. Astronomers can also use the spectrum to find out which different gases make up a cloud of gas, by looking at starlight that has travelled through the cloud.

▶ Astronomers divide stars into classes from O, largest and hottest, to M, smallest and coolest.

O	Blue, very large and hot
B	Blue-white
A	White

ASTRONOMY

264 If a star or galaxy is moving away from Earth, its light is stretched out. This shows up in its spectrum and astronomers call it red shift. They use it to work out how fast a galaxy is moving and how far away it is. If the galaxy is moving towards Earth, the light gets squashed together and shows up in its spectrum as blue shift.

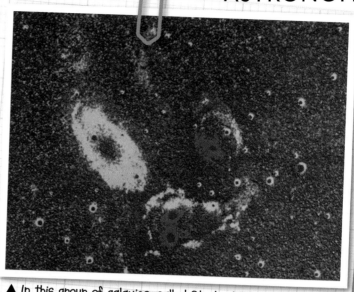

▲ In this group of galaxies, called Stephan's Quintet, the ones that have been coloured red are moving away very quickly.

▼ This diagram shows the light waves coming to Earth from a distant galaxy as a wiggly line.

① A galaxy that stays the same distance from us has a normal spectrum.

② If the galaxy is moving away the light is stretched out and the spectrum shifts towards the red end.

③ If the galaxy is moving nearer the light is squashed up and the spectrum shifts towards the blue end.

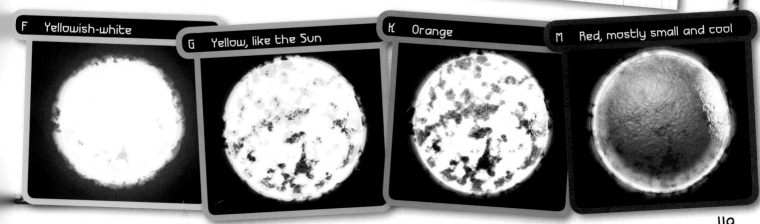

F Yellowish-white

G Yellow, like the Sun

K Orange

M Red, mostly small and cool

119

Space telescopes

265 Galaxies and stars send out other kinds of radiation, as well as light. Some send out radio waves like the ones that carry TV signals. There are also X-rays, like the kind that hospitals use to show broken bones, infrared light, gamma rays and ultra-violet light. They all carry information.

267 The Hubble space telescope is like a normal telescope, but it is above the air. Its images are much clearer than if it were on the ground. It has produced images of distant gas clouds showing star birth, and looked deep into space at galaxies that have never been seen before.

▶ The Hubble space telescope was launched into orbit around the Earth in 1990 and is still sending astronomers amazing images from space.

266 Some kinds of radiation are detected more easily by telescopes in space. This is because the air around Earth stops most radiation from reaching the ground, which is good, because it would be harmful to life on Earth. Space telescopes orbit Earth to collect the radiation and send the information down to Earth.

QUIZ

1. What kind of radiation can spot newborn stars?
2. Which space telescopes collect gamma rays from space?
3. What kind of radiation can spot black holes?

Answers:
1. Infrared radiation
2. The Fermi and Integral Gamma-ray Telescopes 3. X-rays and gamma rays

120

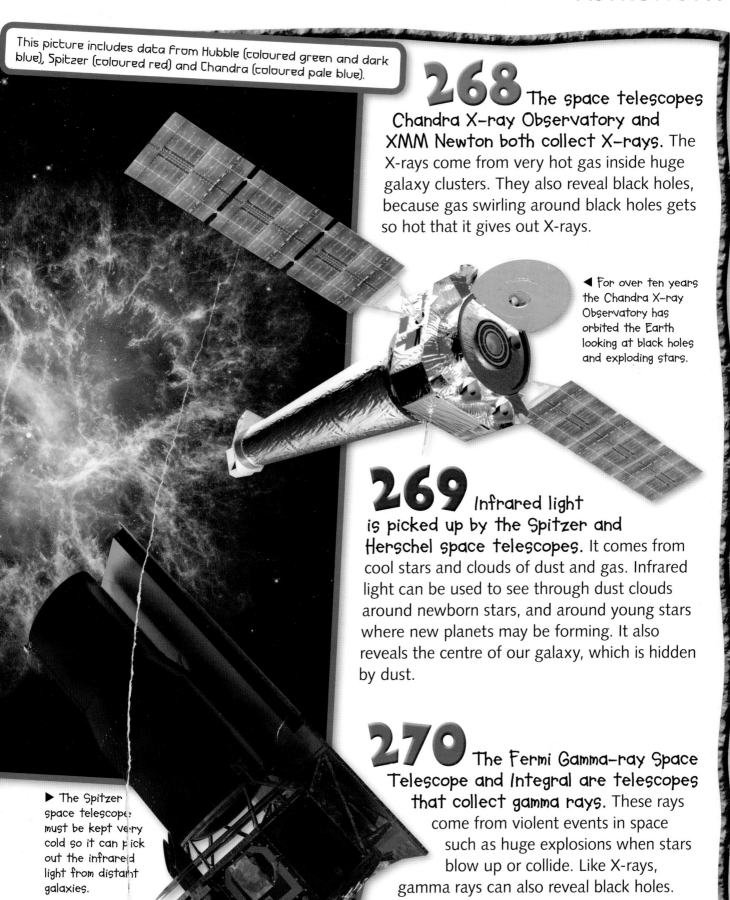

This picture includes data from Hubble (coloured green and dark blue), Spitzer (coloured red) and Chandra (coloured pale blue).

268 The space telescopes Chandra X-ray Observatory and XMM Newton both collect X-rays. The X-rays come from very hot gas inside huge galaxy clusters. They also reveal black holes, because gas swirling around black holes gets so hot that it gives out X-rays.

◀ For over ten years the Chandra X-ray Observatory has orbited the Earth looking at black holes and exploding stars.

269 Infrared light is picked up by the Spitzer and Herschel space telescopes. It comes from cool stars and clouds of dust and gas. Infrared light can be used to see through dust clouds around newborn stars, and around young stars where new planets may be forming. It also reveals the centre of our galaxy, which is hidden by dust.

▶ The Spitzer space telescope must be kept very cold so it can pick out the infrared light from distant galaxies.

270 The Fermi Gamma-ray Space Telescope and Integral are telescopes that collect gamma rays. These rays come from violent events in space such as huge explosions when stars blow up or collide. Like X-rays, gamma rays can also reveal black holes.

Radio telescopes

271 Radio waves from space are collected by radio telescopes. Most radio waves can travel through the air, so these telescopes are built on the ground. But there are lots of radio waves travelling around the Earth, carrying TV and radio signals, and phone calls. These can all interfere with the faint radio waves from space.

272 Radio telescopes work like reflecting telescopes, but instead of using a mirror, waves are collected by a big metal dish. They look like huge satellite TV aerials. Most dishes can turn to point at targets anywhere in the sky, and can track targets moving across the sky.

▶ Each radio telescope dish in the Very Large Array measures 25 metres across and can tilt and turn to face in different directions.

122

I DON'T BELIEVE IT!

Some scientists use radio telescopes to listen out for messages from aliens on other planets or in other galaxies. They have not found any yet.

273 We can't see radio waves, but astronomers turn the signals into images we can see. The images from a single radio telescope dish are not very detailed but several radio telescopes linked together can reveal finer details. The Very Large Array (VLA) in New Mexico, USA, has 27 separate dishes arranged in a 'Y' shape, all working together as though it was one huge dish 36 kilometres across.

▶ These two orange blobs are clouds of hot gas on either side of a galaxy. They are invisible to ordinary telescopes but radio telescopes can reveal them.

274 Radio waves come from cool gas between the stars. This gas is not hot enough to glow so it can't be seen by ordinary telescopes. Radio telescopes have mapped clouds of gas showing the shape of the Milky Way Galaxy. They have also discovered what seems to be a massive black hole at its centre.

275 Radio waves reveal massive jets of gas shooting out from distant galaxies. The jets are thrown out by giant black holes in the middle of some galaxies, which are gobbling up stars and gas around them.

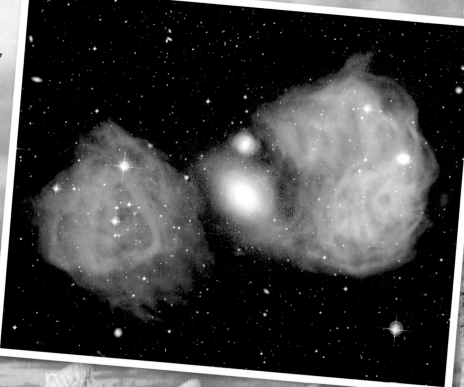

Watching the Sun

276 The Sun is our closest star and astronomers study it to learn about other stars. Without the Sun's light and heat nothing could live on the Earth, so astronomers keep a close eye on it. Tongues of very hot gas called flares and prominences often shoot out from the Sun.

▼ A loop of glowing gas called a prominence **1** arches away from the Sun. Sun spots **2** look dark because they are cooler than the rest of the surface.

277 Particles constantly stream out from the surface of the Sun in all directions. This is called the solar wind. Sometimes a huge burst of particles, called a Coronal Mass Ejection (CME), breaks out. If one comes towards Earth it could damage satellites and even telephone and power lines. CMEs can be dangerous for astronauts in space.

278 There are often dark patches on the Sun. These are cooler areas, and are called sunspots. The number of sunspots changes over time. Every 11 years numbers increase to a maximum of 100 or more, then in between the numbers go down to very few, or even none.

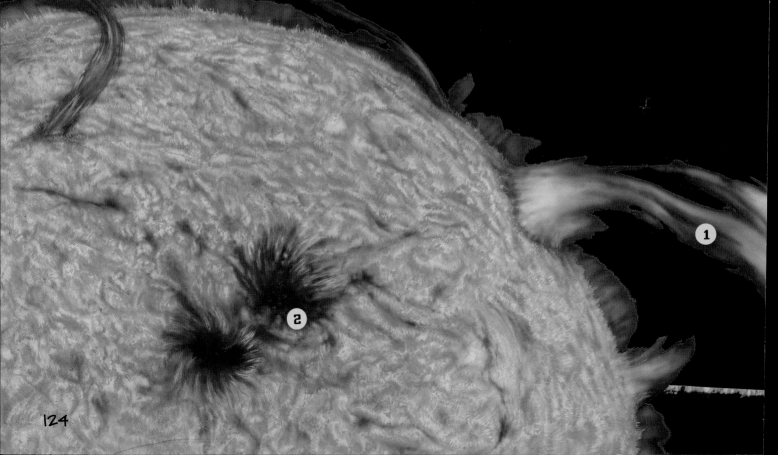

◀ ❶ Wispy gas surrounds the Sun (coloured blue) in this image from the SOHO spacecraft. ❷ SOHO captures a Coronal Mass Ejection exploding out from the Sun.

279 A spacecraft called SOHO has been watching the Sun since 1995. It orbits the Sun between the Earth and the Sun, sending data and images back to Earth. It warns of changes in solar wind and of CMEs that could hit Earth, and has spotted many comets crashing into the Sun.

I DON'T BELIEVE IT!
The Sun is losing weight! Every second about 4 million tonnes of its gas is turned into energy and escapes as light and heat. The Sun is so big that it can continue losing weight at this rate for about another 5 billion years.

280 STEREO are a pair of spacecraft that look at the Sun. They orbit the Sun, one each side of the Earth, to get a 3D view. Like SOHO, they are looking for storms on the Sun that could affect the Earth. Information from STEREO is helping astronomers to work out why these storms happen.

▶ This illustration shows the two Stereo spacecraft soon after they were launched in 2006. They moved apart until they were on either side of the Earth.

The edge of the Universe

281 Astronomers think that the Universe started in a huge explosion they call the Big Bang. They know that distant galaxies are all moving further apart so the Universe must have been squashed tightly together billions of years ago. They think that some kind of explosion sent everything flying apart about 13.7 billion years ago.

282 As astronomers look further away they are also looking back in time. This is because light takes time to travel across the vast distances in space. It takes over four years for light to reach Earth from the second-nearest star (after the Sun), so we see this star as it was when the light left it four years ago. Light can take billions of years to travel from distant galaxies, so astronomers are looking back at the Universe as it was billions of years ago.

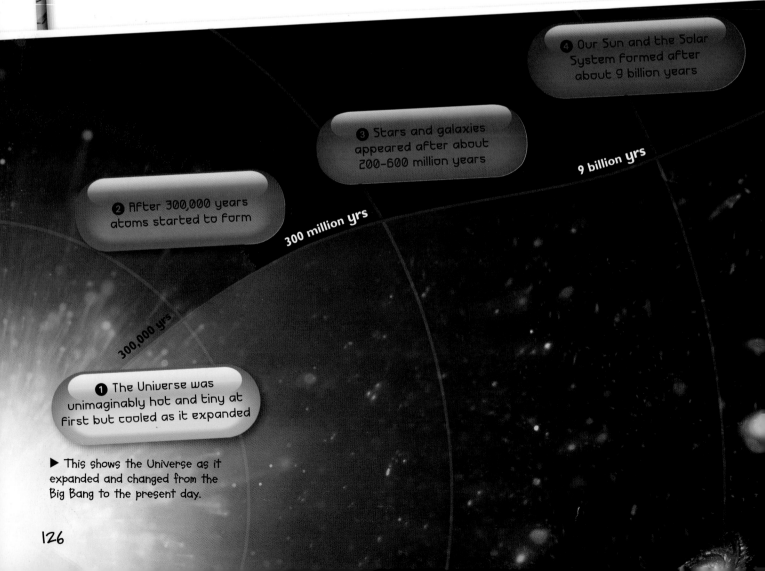

❹ Our Sun and the Solar System formed after about 9 billion years

❸ Stars and galaxies appeared after about 200–600 million years

9 billion yrs

❷ After 300,000 years atoms started to form

300 million yrs

300,000 yrs

❶ The Universe was unimaginably hot and tiny at first but cooled as it expanded

▶ This shows the Universe as it expanded and changed from the Big Bang to the present day.

◀ A map of the Cosmic Background Radiation shows tiny differences in temperature, the red areas are slightly warmer and the blue areas cooler.

283 Astronomers have found faint radiation coming from all over the sky. They call this the Cosmic Background Radiation. It is the remains of radiation left by the Big Bang explosion and helps to prove that the Big Bang really happened. Astronomers send satellites up to map this radiation and find out more about the Universe when it was very young.

13.7 billion yrs

5 The Universe is now about 13.7 billion years old

▲ These galaxies are so far away that we are seeing them as they were billions of years ago when the Universe was much younger.

284 Astronomers use their biggest telescopes and space telescopes to try and find the most distant galaxies. They do not know how soon after the Big Bang the first stars and galaxies appeared and whether they were different from the stars and galaxies they see today. The Hubble space telescope has taken images of very faint faraway galaxies showing astronomers what the early Universe was like.

Up close

285
The planets and our Moon have all been explored by space probes. These travel through space carrying cameras and other instruments with which they can gather data. They then send all the information and images back to astronomers on Earth.

286
Some space probes fly past planets, gathering information. The Voyager 2 space probe flew past the four giant planets (Jupiter, Saturn, Uranus and Neptune) in turn between 1979 and 1989. Astronomers now know much more about these planets from the detailed information and images Voyager 2 sent back.

VOYAGER 2

▶ Voyager 2 sent back this picture of Callisto, one of Jupiter's large moons.

Launch date: 20 August, 1977
Mission: Flew past Jupiter in 1979, Saturn in 1981, Uranus in 1986 and Neptune in 1989. Now flying out of the Solar System into deep space.

287

Space probes can orbit a planet to study it for longer. The probe *Cassini* went into orbit round Saturn. It carried a smaller probe that dropped onto Saturn's largest moon, Titan, to look at its surface, which is hidden by cloud. The main probe circled Saturn, investigating its moons and rings.

288

Venus is hidden by clouds, but the *Magellan* probe was able to map its surface. The probe sent radio signals through the clouds to bounce off the surface. It then collected the return signal. This is called radar. It revealed that Venus has many volcanoes.

CASSINI

▶ Saturn and its rings, taken by the *Cassini* spacecraft as it approached the planet.

Launch date: 15 October, 1997
Mission: Arrived at Saturn in 2004. Dropped Huygens probe onto Saturn's largest moon, Titan, then went into orbit to explore Saturn, its rings and moons.

289

Some probes land on a planet's surface. The probes *Spirit* and *Opportunity* explored the surface of Mars. They move slowly, stopping to take pictures and analyze rocks. They have discovered that although Mars is very dry now, there may have once been water on the surface.

SPIRIT AND OPPORTUNITY

Launch date: 10 June, 2003 (Spirit) and 7 July, 2003 (Opportunity)
Mission: After landing on Mars in January 2004 the two rovers drove across the surface testing the rocks and soil and sending back images and data.

▲ Among the many rocks scattered across the dusty Martian landscape *Spirit* found a rock that could have crashed down from space.

Astronomy from home

290 Many people enjoy astronomy as a hobby. You need warm clothes and somewhere dark, away from street and house lights, and a clear night. After about half an hour your eyes adjust to the dark so you can see more stars. A map of the constellations will help you find your way around the night sky.

291 Binoculars reveal even more stars and show details on the Moon. It is best to look at the Moon when it is half full. Craters, where rocks have crashed into the Moon, show up along the dark edge down the middle of the Moon. Binoculars also show Jupiter's moons as spots of light on or either side of the planet.

292 Telescopes are usually more powerful than binoculars and show fainter stars. They also show more detail in faint gas clouds called nebulae. Amateurs use reflecting and refracting telescopes, mounted on stands to keep them steady.

293 A camera can be fixed to a telescope to photograph the sky. A camera can build up an image over time if the telescope moves to follow the stars. The images show details that you could not see by just looking through the telescope.

KIT LIST
* Star map
* Red light torch
* Deckchair
* Warm clothes
* Pencil and notebook
* Blanket or sleeping bag
* Binoculars
* Telescope

SPOT VENUS
Venus is the brightest planet and easy to spot – it is known as the 'evening star'. Look towards the west in the twilight just after the Sun has set. The first bright 'star' to appear will often be Venus.

▼ In November each year amateur astronomers look out for extra shooting stars during the Leonid meteor shower.

▲ In 1997 the bright Comet Hale Bopp could be seen easily without a telescope or binoculars.

294 **Meteors, also called shooting stars, look like streaks of light in the sky.** They are made when tiny pieces of space rock and dust hit the air around the Earth and burn up. Several times during the year there are meteor showers when many shooting stars are seen. You can spot meteors without a telescope or binoculars.

▶ An amateur astronomer uses binoculars to see the many stars in the Milky Way.

295 **Amateurs can collect useful information for professional astronomers.** They are often the first to spot a new comet in the sky. Comets are named after the person who found them and some amateur astronomers even specialize in comet-spotting. Others watch variable stars and keep records of the changes in their brightness.

In the future

296
Kepler is a satellite built specially to look for stars that might have planets where there could be life. So far, astronomers have not found life anywhere else in the Solar System. Kepler was launched in 2009 and is looking at stars to see if any of them have any planets like Earth.

▶ A Delta II rocket launches the Kepler spacecraft in March 2009 on its mission to hunt for distant planets.

I DON'T BELIEVE IT!
Astronomers are planning a new radio telescope, to be built in either Australia or South Africa. It is called the Square Kilometre Array and will have at least 3000 separate radio telescopes. It should start working in 2020.

297
ALMA (short for Atacama Large Millimetre Array) is a powerful radio telescope built high up in the Atacama Desert in Chile. It has 66 radio dishes linked together to make one huge radio telescope.

298

The James Webb Space Telescope will replace the Hubble Space telescope in 2018. Its mirror will be 6.5 metres across, nearly three times wider than Hubble's main mirror. This will not fit in a rocket so it will be made of 18 separate mirrors that will unfold and fit together once the telescope is in space.

▲ A large sunshield will keep the mirrors of the James Webb telescope cool so it can make images using infrared light.

299

Several new giant telescopes are being planned. The Thirty Meter Telescope will have a mirror 30 metres across – about the length of three double-decker buses. This will be made of 492 smaller mirrors. The European Extremely Large Telescope will have an even larger mirror, 42 metres across, made of 984 separate mirrors. Both should be ready to use in 2018.

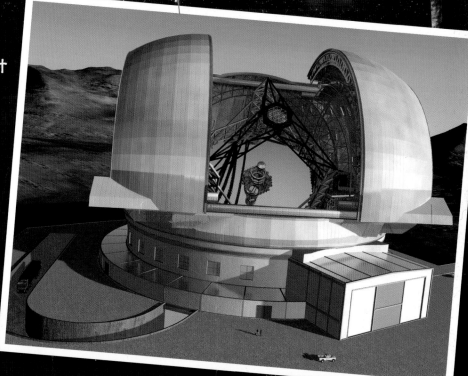

▲ The European

301 For thousands of years people gazed up at the night sky and wondered what it would be like to explore space. This became a reality around 50 years ago, and since then humans have been to the Moon, and unmanned spacecraft have visited all of the planets in the Solar System. Spacecraft have also explored other planets' moons, asteroids and glowing comets. These amazing discoveries help us to understand the Universe.

▶ ESA's *Integral* satellite (launched in 2002) is deployed from a Proton rocket to observe invisible gamma rays in space. Since 1957, humans have sent spacecraft to all eight planets in the Solar System, as well as more than 50 moons, asteroids and comets.

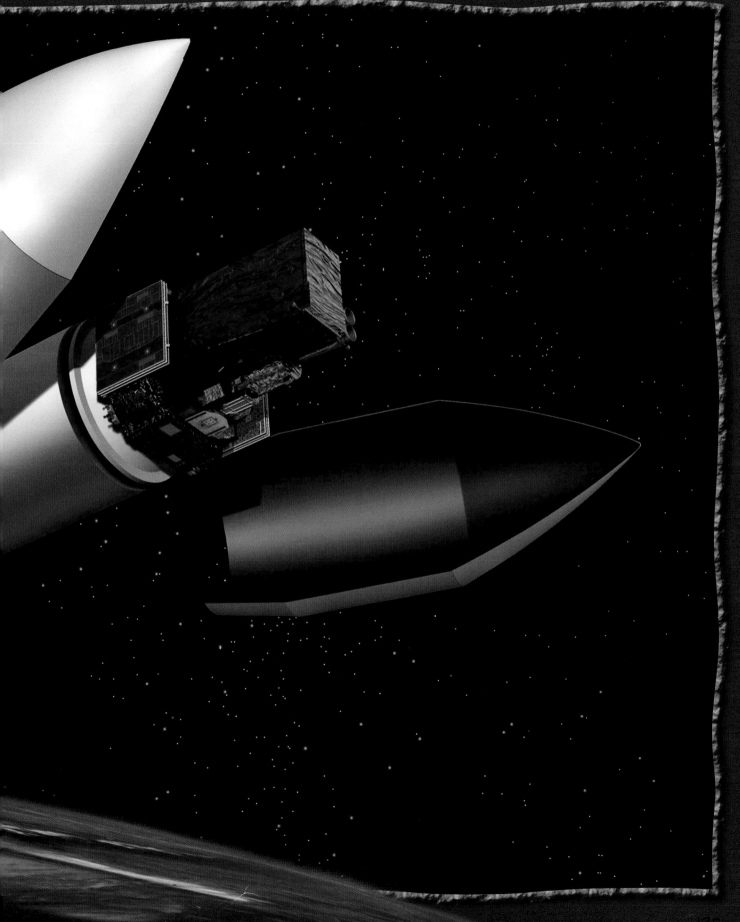

Who explores, and why?

302 Exploring space involves sending craft, robots, equipment and sometimes people to planets, moons, asteroids and comets. Some craft fly near to their targets, while others land. As they explore, they gather information to send back to Earth.

303 Space exploration is different from other space sciences. For example, astronomy is the study of objects in space including planets, stars and galaxies, as well as the Universe as a whole. Much of this is done using telescopes, rather than travelling out into space.

Vandenberg Air Force Base and Spaceport, California, USA

NORTH AMERICA

NASA Headquarters, Washington D.C., USA

Kennedy Space, Center, Florida, USA

Alcantara Launch Center, Sao Luis, Brazil

Guiana Space Centre, Kourou, French Guiana

SOUTH AMERICA

▼ Astronomers use huge, extremely powerful telescopes to observe outer space from Earth.

▲ Space mission headquarters and launch sites are spread across the world.

304 Space exploration is complicated and expensive. Generally, only large nations, such as the USA, Russia, Japan and Europe, send craft into space. Recently, China and India have also launched exploratory missions.

305

Sending even a small spacecraft into space costs vast amounts of money. The Japanese *Hayabusa* mission to bring back samples of the comet Itokawa began in 2003. It lasted seven years and cost around $170 million. Sending the *Phoenix* lander to Mars in 2008 was even more expensive, at $450 million dollars.

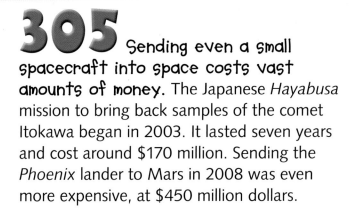

▶ The comet-visiting *Hayabusa* spacecraft blasted off from Uchinoura Space Centre, Japan, in 2003. It returned to Earth in 2010, carrying samples of comet dust.

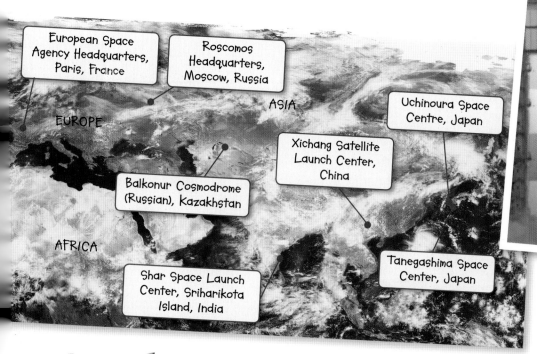

European Space Agency Headquarters, Paris, France

Roscomos Headquarters, Moscow, Russia

ASIA

EUROPE

Uchinoura Space Centre, Japan

Xichang Satellite Launch Center, China

Balkonur Cosmodrome (Russian), Kazakhstan

AFRICA

Shar Space Launch Center, Sriharikota Island, India

Tanegashima Space Center, Japan

▼ Recent observations in space suggest faraway stars could have planets forming around them from bits of gas, dust and rock – similiar to our own Solar System.

306

If the costs are so great, why do we explore space? Exploring the unknown has long been a part of human nature. Space exploration provides clues that may help us to understand how the Universe formed. Progress in space technology can also help advances on Earth.

Early explorers

307 The Space Age began in 1957 when Russia launched *Sputnik 1*, the first Earth-orbiting satellite. It was a metal, ball-shaped craft that could measure pressure and temperature, and send radio signals back to Earth.

▼ Tracking *Sputnik 1*'s orbit showed how the upper atmosphere of the Earth fades into space.

308 In 1958, the USA launched the satellite *Explorer 1*. As it orbited the Earth it detected two doughnut-shaped belts of high-energy particles, known as the Van Allen Belts. They can damage spacecraft and interfere with radio signals.

◄ The Van Allen belts are made up of particles, trapped by Earth's natural magnetic field.

Inner belt

Outer belt

309 In 1959, Russia's *Luna 1* spacecraft was aiming for the Moon, but it missed. Later that year, *Luna 2* crashed into the Moon on purpose, becoming the first craft to reach another world. On its way down the craft measured the Moon's gravity and magnetism.

Heat-resistant outer casing

Inner casing

Batteries

Antennae

Ventilation fan

QUIZ

Early exploration was a 'Space Race' between the USA and the Soviet Union. Which had these 'firsts'?

1. First satellite in space
2. First person in space
3. First craft on the Moon
4. First person on the Moon

Answers:
1, 2, 3 – Russia 4 – USA

Hatch

Heat shield covering

Long range antenna

◀ Gagarin's *Vostok 1* spacecraft was ten times larger than the *Sputnik 1* satellite, and 50 times heavier.

Descent module – only this ball-shaped part came back to Earth

Oxygen and nitrogen gas tanks for fuel and for Gagarin to breathe

Retro-thruster

310
The first person in space was Russian cosmonaut Yuri Gagarin. In 1961 he made one orbit of Earth in the spacecraft *Vostok 1*. The furthest he travelled into space was 327 kilometres. Gagarin's trip made news around the world and showed that humans could survive in space.

311
The US sent seven Surveyor craft to the Moon between 1966 and 1968. Five succeeded in soft-landing (landing without being destroyed) on the surface. This was an important stage in planning the most exciting and ambitious mission of all – sending people to another world.

▶ *Surveyor 3* landed on the Moon in April 1967. It was photographed by the *Apollo 12* astronauts in November 1969.

Man on the Moon!

312 The only humans to have explored another world are 12 US astronauts that were part of the Apollo program. Six Apollo missions landed on the Moon between 1969 and 1972, each with two astronauts. First to step onto the surface were Neil Armstrong and Buzz Aldrin from *Apollo 11*, on 20 July, 1969.

313 Each Apollo lunar lander touched down on a different type of terrain. The astronauts stayed on the Moon for three or four days. They explored, carried out experiments and collected samples of Moon dust and rocks to bring back to Earth.

314 The last three Apollo missions took a Lunar Roving Vehicle (LRV), or 'Moon buggy'. The astronauts drove for up to 20 kilometres at a time, exploring the Moon's hills, valleys, flat plains and cliffs.

315 Since the Apollo missions, more than 50 unmanned spacecraft have orbited or landed on the Moon. In 1994, US orbiter *Clementine* took many photographs, gravity readings and detailed maps of the Moon's surface.

◄ *Apollo 15's Lunar Module pilot James Irwin salutes the US flag and his Commander David Scott, in 1971. Their Lunar Module lander is behind and the Moon buggy is to the right.*

MISSION	DATE	CREW	ACHIEVEMENT
Apollo 11	July 1969	Neil Armstrong (C) Buzz Aldrin (LMP) Michael Collins (CMP)	First humans on another world
Apollo 12	November 1969	Pete Conrad (C) Alan Bean (LMP) Richard Gordon (CMP)	First colour television pictures of the Moon returned to Earth
Apollo 13	April 1970	James Lovell (C) Fred Haise (LMP) Jack Swigert (CMP)	Apollo 13 turned back after launch because of an explosion. It never reached the Moon, but returned safely to Earth
Apollo 14	January–February 1971	Alan Shepard (C) Edgar Mitchell (LMP) Stuart Roosa (CMP)	Longest Moon walks in much improved spacesuits
Apollo 15	July–August 1971	David Scott (C) James Irwin (LMP) Alfred Worden (CMP)	First use of a Moon buggy allowed astronauts to explore a wider range
Apollo 16	April 1972	John Young (C) Charles Duke (LMP) Thomas Mattingly (CMP)	First and only mission to land in the Moon's highlands
Apollo 17	December 1972	Eugene Cernan (C) Harrison Schmitt (LMP) Ronald Evans (CMP)	Returned a record 49 kilograms of rock and dust samples

316 In 2009, the *Lunar Reconnaissance Orbiter* began mapping the Moon's surface in detail. Its pictures showed parts of the Apollo craft left by the astronauts. In the same year the Indian orbiter *Chandrayaan 1* discovered ice on the Moon.

◄ On each mission, the Commander (C) and the Lunar Module pilot (LMP) landed on the Moon, while the Command Module pilot (CMP) stayed in the orbiting craft.

Plan and prepare

317 Planning a mission takes many years. Scientists suggest places to explore, what might be discovered, and the cost. Their government must agree for the mission to go ahead.

▲ In 1961 US space engineer John Houbolt developed the idea of using a three-part spacecraft for the Apollo Moon missions.

318 There are many types of exploratory missions. A flyby takes the spacecraft near to its target world, and past. An orbiter circles around the target. A lander mission touches down on the surface. A lander may release a rover, which can travel around on the surface.

▲ For worlds with an atmosphere, parachutes are used to lower a lander gently. This parachute design for a planned mission to Mars is being tested in the world's biggest wind tunnel in California, USA.

319 The ever-changing positions of Earth and other objects in space mean there is a limited 'launch window' for each mission. This is when Earth is in the best position for a craft to reach its target in the shortest time. If the launch window is missed, the distances may become too massive.

▼ The *New Horizons* spacecraft was assembled and checked in perfectly clean, dust-free conditions before being launched to Pluto in 2006.

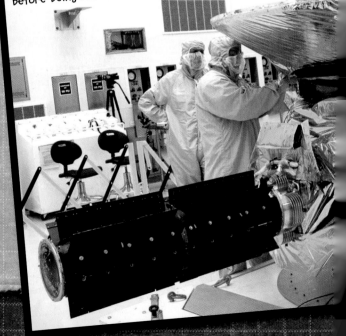

320 In space, repairs are difficult or impossible. Exploring craft must be incredibly reliable, with tested and proven technology. Each piece of equipment needs a back-up, and even if this fails, it should not affect other parts.

321 A spacecraft must be able to cope with the conditions in space and on other worlds. It is incredibly cold in space, but planets such as Venus are hotter than boiling water. Other planets have hazards such as clouds made of tiny drops of acid.

▶ The spacecraft *Galileo* was tested in ultra-bright light of the same level that it would receive as it flew nearer the Sun in 1990 on its way to Jupiter.

322 A test version of the spacecraft is tried on Earth. If successful, the real craft is built in strict conditions. One loose screw or speck of dust could cause disaster. There's no second chance once the mission begins.

Blast-off!

323 A spacecraft is blasted into space by its launch vehicle, or rocket. The rocket is the only machine powerful enough to reach 'escape velocity' – the speed needed to break free from the pull of Earth's gravity. The spacecraft is usually folded up in the nose cone of the rocket.

324 Different sizes of rockets are used for different sizes of spacecraft. One of the heaviest was the *Cassini-Huygens* mission to Saturn. At its launch in 1997, with all its fuel and equipment on board, it weighed 5.6 tonnes – almost as much as a school bus. It needed a huge *Titan IV* rocket launcher to power it into space.

325 Spacecraft and other objects carried by the rocket are called the 'payload'. Most rockets take their payload into orbit around the Earth. The nose cone opens to release the craft stored inside. Parts of it unfold, such as the solar panels that turn sunlight into electricity.

Launch point

Escape velocity

Orbit bound by Earth's gravity

◀ Launch vehicles must quickly reach escape velocity – 11,200 metres per second – to shrug off Earth's gravitational pull.

SECOND STAGE (S-II)
The middle section of the launcher had five J-2 rocket engines. It was 25 metres tall, and like the first stage, was 10 metres wide.

FIRST STAGE (S-IC)
The bottom part of *Saturn V* was 42 metres tall. The F-1 rocket engines propelled the entire launch vehicle for the first 60 kilomentres.

J-2 rocket engines

F-1 rocket engines

▲ The biggest launchers were the three-stage *Saturn V* rockets used to launch the Apollo missions. Each stage fell away after using up its fuel.

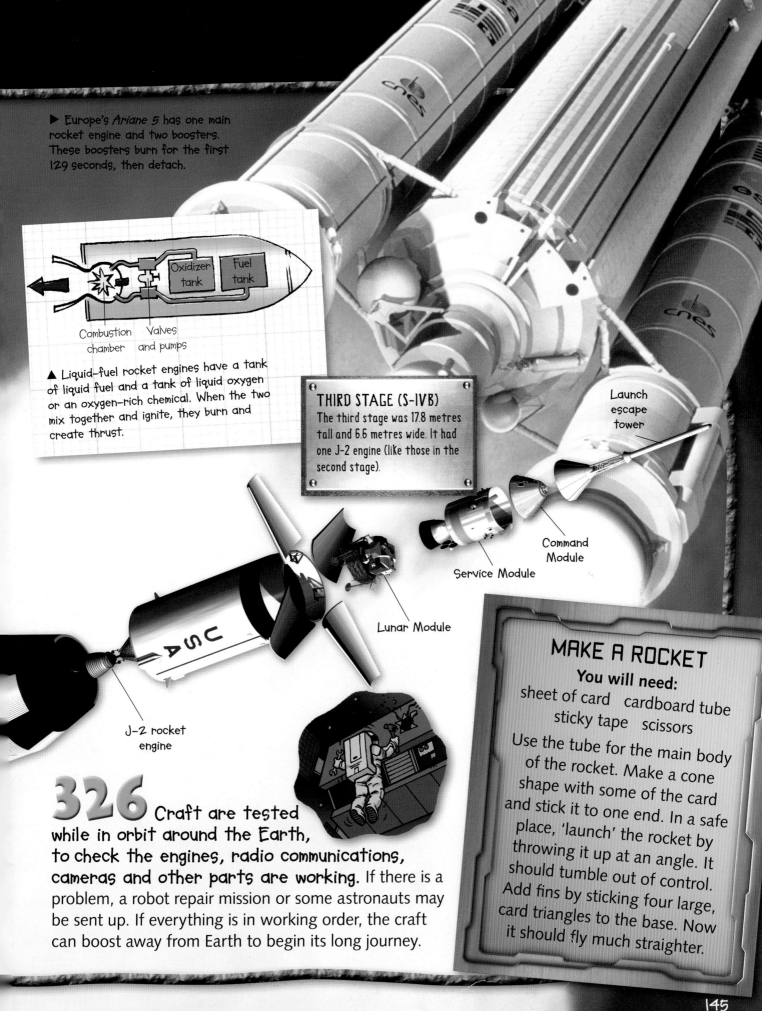

▶ Europe's *Ariane 5* has one main rocket engine and two boosters. These boosters burn for the first 129 seconds, then detach.

Oxidizer tank

Fuel tank

Combustion chamber

Valves and pumps

▲ Liquid-fuel rocket engines have a tank of liquid fuel and a tank of liquid oxygen or an oxygen-rich chemical. When the two mix together and ignite, they burn and create thrust.

THIRD STAGE (S-IVB)
The third stage was 17.8 metres tall and 6.6 metres wide. It had one J-2 engine (like those in the second stage).

Launch escape tower

Command Module

Service Module

Lunar Module

J-2 rocket engine

326 Craft are tested while in orbit around the Earth, to check the engines, radio communications, cameras and other parts are working. If there is a problem, a robot repair mission or some astronauts may be sent up. If everything is in working order, the craft can boost away from Earth to begin its long journey.

MAKE A ROCKET
You will need:
sheet of card   cardboard tube   sticky tape   scissors

Use the tube for the main body of the rocket. Make a cone shape with some of the card and stick it to one end. In a safe place, 'launch' the rocket by throwing it up at an angle. It should tumble out of control. Add fins by sticking four large, card triangles to the base. Now it should fly much straighter.

In deep space

327 Most spacecraft travel for months, even years, to their destinations. The fastest journey to Mars took just over six months, by *Mars Express* in 2003. *Pioneer 10* took 11 years to reach Neptune in 1983.

◀ *Mars Express* cruised at a speed of 10,800 kilometres an hour on its way to Mars.

328 Guiding the craft on its course is vital. A tiny error could mean that it misses its distant target by millions of kilometres. Mission controllers on Earth regularly check the craft's position with radio signals using the Deep Space Network (DSN). The DSN is made up of three huge radio dishes located in California, USA, Madrid in Spain, and Canberra, Australia.

▼ This ion thruster is being tested in a vacuum chamber. The blue glow is the beam of charged atoms being thrown out of the engine.

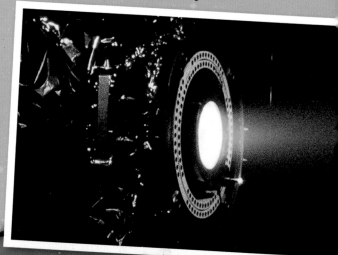

329 Spacecraft only need small engines because there is no air in space to slow them down. Depending on the length of the journey, different kinds of engines and fuels are used. The ion thruster uses magnetism made by electricity. This hurls tiny particles, called ions, backwards, which pushes the craft forwards.

◄ Bowl-shaped antennae (aerials), like *New Horizons'*, exchange radio signals to and from Earth.

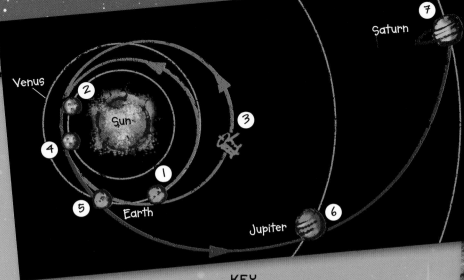

▲ *Cassini–Huygens'* journey to Saturn involved four gravity-assists. The main stages were: launch to first Venus flyby (orange), second Venus flyby (blue), and Earth flyby, past Jupiter to Saturn (purple).

330

Craft often pass other planets or moons on their journeys. Like Earth, these objects all have a gravitational pull, and this could send a craft off course. However, a planet's gravity may be used to propel the craft in a new direction to save fuel. This is known as a gravity-assisted flyby or 'slingshot'.

KEY

❶ October 1997 Launch from Earth

❷ April 1998 First Venus flyby

❸ December 1998 Engine fires for 90 minutes to return to Venus

❹ June 1999 Second Venus flyby

❺ August 1999 Earth-Moon flyby

❻ December 2000 Jupiter flyby

❼ July 2004 Arrives in orbit around Saturn

Goldstone, California, USA

◄ ▼ The three Deep Space Network sites are equally spaced around Earth, with 120 degrees between them, making a 360-degree circle.

Madrid, Spain

Canberra, Australia

331

For long periods, much of a craft's equipment shuts down to save electricity. It's like an animal hibernating in winter or a mobile phone on stand-by. When the craft 'hibernates' only a few vital systems stay active, such as navigation.

► The Deep Space Network's radio dish at Goldstone near Barstow, California, is 70 metres across.

332 As the spacecraft approaches its target, its systems power up and it 'comes to life'. Controllers on Earth test the craft's radio communications and other equipment. At such enormous distances, radio signals can take minutes, even hours, to make the journey.

333 Among the most important devices onboard a craft are cameras. Some work like telescopes to take a close-up or magnified view of a small area. Others are wide-angle cameras, which capture a much greater area without magnifying.

334 Other kinds of camera can 'see' types of waves that are invisible to the human eye. These include infrared or heat rays, ultraviolet rays, radio waves and X-rays. These rays and waves provide information about the target world, such as how hot or cold it is.

▼ *Mars Reconnaissance Orbiter*'s photograph of the 730-metre-wide Victoria Crater was captured by its high-resolution camera and shows amazing detail.

The Mars Climate Sounder records the temperature, moisture and dust in the Martian atmosphere

The high-resolution camera captures close-up, detailed photographs of the surface

QUIZ

Spacecraft have many devices, but rarely microphones to detect sound. Why?

A. The chance of meeting aliens who can shout loudly is very small.
B. Sound waves do not travel through the vacuum of space.
C. It's too difficult to change sound waves into radio signals.

Answer:
B

Antenna

335 Magnetometers detect magnetic fields, which exist naturally around some planets, including Earth. Gravitometers measure the target object's pull of gravity. This is especially important in the final stage of the journey – the landing. Some spacecraft also have space dust collectors.

Solar panel

◄ *Mars Reconnaissance Orbiter*, launched in 2005, carries a telescopic camera, wide–angle cameras, sensors for infrared and ultraviolet light and a radar that 'sees' below the surface.

The spectrometer identifies different substances on the surface by measuring how much light is reflected

The sub-surface radar can see up to one kilometre below the planet's surface

336 The information from the cameras and sensors is turned into radio signal codes and beamed back to Earth. To send and receive these signals, the craft has one or more dish-shaped antennae. These must be in the correct position to communicate with the dishes located on Earth.

Flyby, bye-bye

337 On a flyby mission, a spacecraft comes close to its target. It does not go into orbit around it or land – it flies onwards and away into deep space. Some flybys are part of longer missions to even more distant destinations. In these cases the flyby may also involve gravity assist.

LAUNCH FROM EARTH 20 August, 1977

JUPITER

Flyby on 9 July, 1979

338 A flyby craft may pass its target several times on a long, lop-sided path, before leaving again. Each pass gives a different view of the target object. The craft's cameras, sensors and other equipment switch on to take pictures and record measurements, then turn off again as it flies away.

339 The ultimate flyby craft was *Voyager 2*. It made a 'Grand Tour' of the four outermost planets, which are only suitably aligned every 175 years. *Voyager 2* blasted off in 1977 and flew past Jupiter in 1979, Saturn in 1981, Uranus in 1986 and Neptune in 1989. This craft is still sending back information from a distance twice as far as Pluto is from Earth.

I DON'T BELIEVE IT!
When *Pioneer 11* zoomed to within 43,000 kilometres of Jupiter in 1974, it made the fastest-ever flyby at 50 kilometres per second.

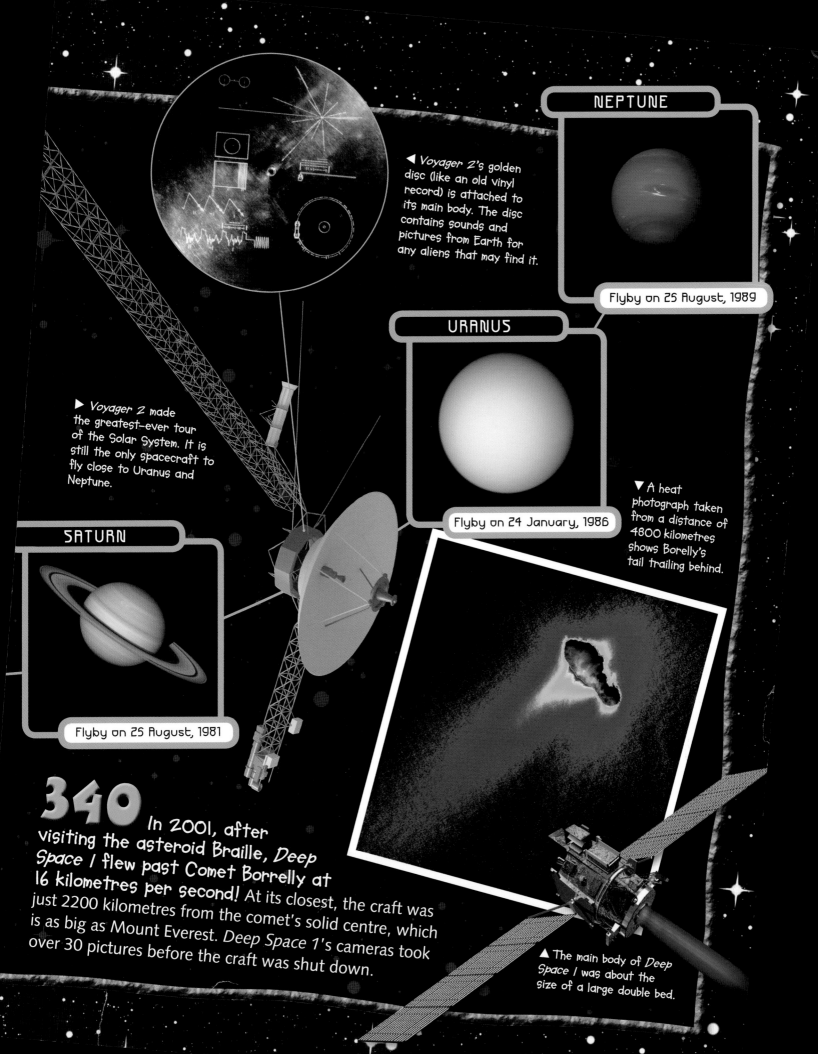

◀ Voyager 2's golden disc (like an old vinyl record) is attached to its main body. The disc contains sounds and pictures from Earth for any aliens that may find it.

NEPTUNE

Flyby on 25 August, 1989

URANUS

▶ Voyager 2 made the greatest-ever tour of the Solar System. It is still the only spacecraft to fly close to Uranus and Neptune.

Flyby on 24 January, 1986

▼ A heat photograph taken from a distance of 4800 kilometres shows Borelly's tail trailing behind.

SATURN

Flyby on 25 August, 1981

340 In 2001, after visiting the asteroid Braille, *Deep Space 1* flew past Comet Borrelly at 16 kilometres per second! At its closest, the craft was just 2200 kilometres from the comet's solid centre, which is as big as Mount Everest. *Deep Space 1*'s cameras took over 30 pictures before the craft was shut down.

▲ The main body of *Deep Space 1* was about the size of a large double bed.

Into orbit

341 On many exploring missions the craft is designed to go into orbit around its target world. Craft that do this are called orbiters, and they provide a much longer, closer look than a flyby mission.

▶ There are several different types of orbit that craft can make around their targets. Here, they are shown around Earth.

A polar orbit passes over the North and South Poles

An equatorial orbit goes around the middle (Equator)

Most orbits are elliptical, with low and high points

342 One of the most elliptical orbits was made by *Mars Global Surveyor*. At its closest, it passed Mars at a distance of 171 kilometres, twice in each orbit. The craft's furthest distance away was more than ten times greater.

◀ In 2006, two twin STEREO-craft went into orbit around the Sun. With one in front and one behind Earth, the craft made the first 3D observations of the Sun.

Antenna

ORBITER
You will need:
sock   tennis ball   string (one metre long)

Put the ball in the sock and tie up the top with the string. Go outside. Holding the string half way along its length, whirl the sock above your head so that it 'orbits' you. Gradually lengthen the string – does the 'orbit' take longer?

DIONE

During its orbits of Saturn, Cassini passed Dione, Saturn's 15th largest moon. Saturn can be seen in the distance.

343 The *Cassini* orbiter, part of the *Cassini–Huygens* mission, has been through many changes of orbit around Saturn. Some went close to the main planet and some passed near to its rings. Other orbits took it past Saturn's largest moon, Titan, and its smaller moons, including Enceladus, Iapetus and Mimas.

344 A spacecraft's radar checks its average height above the surface. Radio or microwave signals beam down to the surface and bounce back. The time this takes tells the craft how far away it is. More detailed radar measurements map the surface far below.

Camera

345 A spectrometer analyzes different colours in light waves. Different chemical substances give off or reflect certain colours of light better than others. By reading this, the spectrometer can work out what substances are present in a planet's atmosphere or on its surface.

▶ *Mars Global Surveyor's* average orbital height was 378 kilometres. It mapped the entire Martian surface.

Solar panel

346 The orbiter continually checks and adjusts its height and position. It does this using tiny puffs of gas from its thrusters, which stops the craft losing speed and crashing into the surface.

Landers and impactors

347 Some missions have landers that touch down onto the surface of their target world. Part of the spacecraft may detach and land while the other part stays in orbit, or the whole spacecraft may land.

① Spacecraft in orbit

② Landing module separates from orbiter

③ First parachute opened, then detached

▶ The later landers of the Russian *Venera* program (1961–1983) used parachutes to slow down in the thick, hot, cloudy atmosphere of Venus.

348 The journey down can be hazardous. If the planet has an atmosphere (layer of gas around it) there may be strong winds that could blow the lander off course. If the atmosphere is thick, there may be huge pressure pushing on the craft.

④ Main parachutes opened at a height of 50 kilometres above the surface

349 If there is an atmosphere, the lander may use parachutes, or inflate its own balloons or air bags, to slow its speed. On the *Cassini-Huygens* mission, the *Huygens* lander used two parachutes as it descended for touchdown on Saturn's moon, Titan.

⑤ Ring-shaped shock absorber filled with compressed gas lessened the impact at touchdown

350 If there is no atmosphere, retro-thrusters are used to slow the craft down. These puff gases in the direction of travel. Most landers have a strong, bouncy casing for protection as they hit the surface, or long, springy legs to reduce the impact.

▲ A photograph taken by *Deep Impact* 67 seconds after its impactor crashed into Comet Tempel I, shows material being thrown out.

351 After touchdown, the lander's solar panels and other parts fold out. Its equipment and systems switch on, and it tests its radio communications with the orbiter and sometimes directly with Earth.

▲ *Beagle 2*'s solar panels were designed to fold out. Contact with the lander was lost soon after it detached from its orbiter in 2003. *Beagle 2* was finally found intact on the Martian surface in 2015 – not all of its solar panels had deployed.

Impactor

352 Some craft are designed to smash into their target, and these are called impactors. The crash is observed by the orbiter and may also be watched by controllers on Earth. The dust, rocks and gases given off by an impact provide valuable information about the target object.

Camera

▶ In 2005, *Deep Impact* released its impactor, watched it strike Comet Tempel I and studied the resulting crater.

◀ *Mars Pathfinder* lander being tested on Earth. It used a parachute, retro-thrusters and multi-bubble air bags to land on Mars.

Robotic rovers

353 After touchdown, some landers release small, robotic vehicles called rovers. They have wheels and motors so they can move around on the surface to explore. So far rovers have explored on the Moon and Mars.

Antennae

Laser reflector

Solar panels

▶ In the 1970s, Russia sent two rovers, *Lunokhod 1* and *2*, to the Moon. Each was the size of a large bathtub, weighed almost one tonne and had eight wheels driven by electric motors.

Cameras

Wheels

QUIZ

How were the Mars rovers *Spirit* and *Opportunity* named?

1. Words chosen at random.
2. By a group of space experts.
3. By a 9-year-old girl, who won a competition.

Answer:
3. Siberian-born American schoolgirl Sofi Collis won the 2003 'Name the Rovers' competition.

354 Modern rovers are mostly robotic – self-controlled using onboard computers. This is because of the time delay of radio signals. Even when Earth and Mars are at their closest distance to each other, radio signals take over three minutes to travel one way. If a rover was driven by remote control from Earth, it could have fallen off a cliff long before its onboard cameras relayed images of this.

355 Rovers are designed and tested to survive the conditions on their target world. Scientists know about these conditions from information collected from observations on Earth, and from previous missions. Test rovers are driven on extreme landscapes on Earth to make sure they can handle tricky terrain.

▲ A test version of a new rover destined for Mars, here being tested on the slippery rocks of a beach in Wales, UK.

356 The *Spirit* and *Opportunity* rovers landed on Mars in 2004. They are equipped with cameras that allow them to navigate around obstacles. Heat-sensitive cameras detect levels of heat soaked up by rocks, giving clues to what the rocks are made of. On-board microscopes and agnets gather and study dust particles containing iron.

▶ Twin rovers *Spirit* and *Opportunity* are each about the size of an office desk.

Navcam

Antenna

Main antenna

Solar panels

Mobile arm carries five gadgets including a camera, rock grinder and magnets

Each wheel has an electric motor

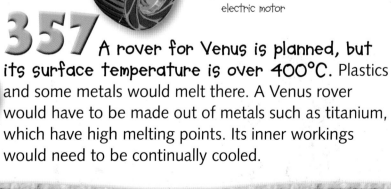

357 A rover for Venus is planned, but its surface temperature is over 400°C. Plastics and some metals would melt there. A Venus rover would have to be made out of metals such as titanium, which have high melting points. Its inner workings would need to be continually cooled.

Close-up look

▶ In the late 1970s the USA's two Viking landers photographed their robotic sampler arms digging into Mars' surface.

358 Some landers and rovers have robot arms that extend from the main body. These scoop or drill into the surface to collect samples, which are then tested in the craft's onboard science laboratory. Samples are tested for chemical reactions, such as bubbling or changing colour.

Solar panel

Robotic arm with scoop and camera

Spheres of minerals containing iron, known as 'blueberries'

Circular area ground by tool is 4.5 centimetres across

359 Most rovers have six wheels. This design allows them to move quickly around sharp corners, without tipping over. Each wheel has an electric motor, powered by onboard batteries that are charged by the solar panels. If the batteries run down, the rover 'sleeps' until light from the Sun recharges them.

◀ Mars rovers *Spirit* and *Opportunity* are both equipped with a rock-grinding tool. They use it to grind into rocks and gather dust samples.

360 The *Phoenix* Mars lander had several devices on its robotic arm to measure features of Martian soil. It measured how easily it carried (conducted) heat and electricity, and if it contained any liquids. *Phoenix* also had microscopes for an ultra-close view of the surface samples.

Meteorological (weather) station

Gas analyzers

Mini science laboratory

Solar panel

361 Most landers and rovers have mini weather stations. Sensors measure temperatures and pressures through the day and night and record the Sun's brightness. They also take samples of gases if there is an atmosphere, and record weather, such as wind and dust storms.

◄ The *Phoenix* Mars lander of 2008 had a robotic arm, on the left, and a small weather station.

362 The orbiting craft acts as a relay station to receive signals from its lander and send them on to Earth. A lander can in turn be a relay station for a rover. A rover has a small radio set to communicate with the lander and the lander has a slightly larger one to communicate with the orbiter. The orbiter has the biggest radio set to communicate with Earth.

▲ In the 1960s five US Surveyor landers sent back separate close-up photographs of the Moon's surface. These were joined together to make larger scenes.

Exploring Mars

363 Mars is the nearest planet to Earth and the most explored. In the 1870s, astronomers thought they could see canals of water on Mars' surface, thought to be built by aliens. But with better telescopes, these 'canals' were found to be simply a trick of the light.

▼ This timeline shows some of the most notable missions in the exploration of Mars.

NOV 1971 *Mariner 9* entered orbit around Mars – the first craft to orbit another planet

DEC 1971 *Mars 3's* lander was the first to touch down safely on Mars, but contact was lost after 20 seconds

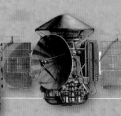

364 Since the 1960s more than 40 missions have set off to Mars. About two-thirds of them failed at launch or on the way. One-quarter have failed at or near Mars, leading some people to believe that Martians were attacking and destroying the craft.

JUL/SEP 1976 *Viking 1 and 2* were the first successful landers on the surface of Mars

JUL 1997 *Mars Pathfinder* landed and released *Sojourner*, the first rover, on another planet

◄ *Mars Odyssey* (2001) produced this image of Mars' south pole. The Martian polar ice caps are made of frozen water and 'dry ice' – solid (frozen) carbon dioxide.

365 In 1976, two US Viking landers carried out research on Mars. They took many photographs, made detailed maps and tested the atmosphere, rocks and soil, but they found no definite signs of life. In 2008, the US *Phoenix* lander discovered water frozen as ice, and many minerals and chemicals in the soil.

366 The *Spirit* and *Opportunity* rovers have made an amazing series of explorations and discoveries. They have found evidence that there was once water on Mars, and that it is possibly still there underground. In 2009 *Spirit* got stuck in soft soil but *Opportunity* is still moving, although very slowly.

MAY 2008 *Phoenix* lander touched down. It was the first craft to land in Mars' polar area

DEC 2003 In orbit, *Mars Express* released its lander, *Beagle 2*, but communications to it were lost

MAR 2006 *Mars Reconnaissance Orbiter* arrived, making a record six working craft in orbit or on the surface of Mars

SEP 1997 *Mars Global Surveyor* went into orbit and began detailed, large-scale mapping of the surface

367 The *Mars Science Laboratory* rover *Curiosity*, which landed in 2012, has a drill, scoop arm and several packages of experiments. It is the biggest-ever rover at almost one tonne in weight. Its aim is to find out if there is, or ever has been, any life on Mars.

JAN 2004 *Mars Exploration Rovers Spirit and Opportunity* arrived on the surface, ready to explore

◄ *Curiosity* is about the size of a Mini car and has a top speed of 2.5 centimetres per second.

368 All spacecraft have a mission control centre on Earth. Expert teams monitor a craft's systems, including radio communications, and the data a craft collects from its cameras and instruments.

▲ Mission controllers at NASA's Jet Propulsion Laboratory in California, USA, celebrate as the first images from rover *Opportunity* reach Earth.

369 Missions often run into problems. Controllers must work out how to keep a mission going when faults occur. If power supplies fail, the teams may have to decide to switch off some equipment so that others can continue working.

370 Sample return missions bring items from space back to Earth. In 2004, the *Genesis* craft dropped off its return container. It was supposed to parachute down to Earth's surface, but it crash-landed in Utah, USA. Luckily, some of its samples of solar wind survived for study.

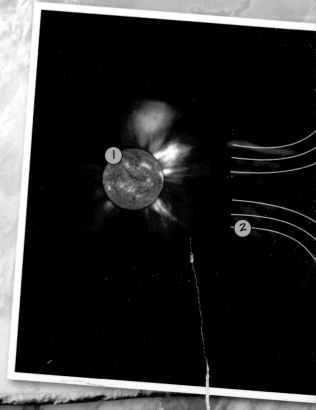

371 Gases, dust, rocks and other items are brought back to Earth to be studied. In the early 1970s the six manned Apollo missions brought a total of 381.7 kilograms of Moon material back to Earth.

▲ This piece of basalt Moon rock, brought back by *Apollo 15*, is being studied by *Apollo 17* astronaut and geologist (rock expert) Jack Schmitt.

372 Samples returned from space must not be contaminated with material from Earth. Keeping samples clean allows scientists to find out what they contain, and stops any dangerous substances being released on Earth. Spacecraft are ultra-clean at launch to prevent them spreading chemicals or germs from Earth to other worlds.

▼ *Genesis* collected high-energy particles from the Sun's solar wind, which distorts Earth's magnetic field.

I DON'T BELIEVE IT!

Moon rocks don't look very special, yet over 100 small ones brought back by the Apollo missions have been stolen. More than ten people have been caught trying to sell them.

▶ This sample of Moon rock collected during the *Apollo 11* mission is housed inside a securely fastened, airtight container.

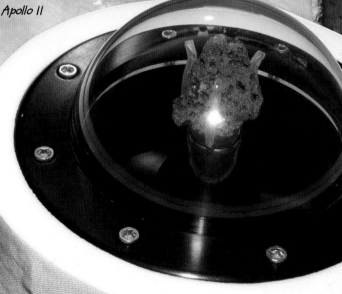

KEY
❶ Sun
❷ Solar wind
❸ Bow shock (where the solar wind meets Earth's magnetic field)
❹ Earth's magnetic field
❺ Earth

◀ This photograph taken by SOHO uses a disc with a hole to block out some of the Sun's glare. This reveals vast streaming clouds of superheated matter called plasma.

Corona

Coronal mass ejection (CME) of superheated

373 Missions to the Sun encounter enormous heat. In the 1970s the US-German craft *Helios 2* flew to within 44 million kilometres of the Sun. From 1990, the *Ulysses* probe travelled on a huge orbit, passing near the Sun and as far out as Jupiter.

374 In 1996, the *SOHO* satellite began studying the Sun from near Earth. Since then, it has found many new comets. In 2015, *Solar Probe Plus* will orbit to within six million kilometres of the Sun, with a shield-like 'sunshade' of heat-resistant, carbon-composite material for protection.

1c

HELIOS MISSION

GRENADA

◀ The Helios mission was featured on stamps worldwide.

▲ *Messenger* had a 'sunshade' made out of a ceramic–composite material to protect it from the Sun's heat.

376 Mercury, the nearest planet to the Sun, has been visited by two spacecraft, *Mariner 10* in 1974, and *Messenger* in 2004. *Messenger* made flybys in 2008 and 2009 and went into orbit in 2011. These craft measured Mercury's surface temperature at 420°C – twice as hot as a home oven.

377 More than 20 craft have visited Venus, the second planet from the Sun. Its atmosphere of thick clouds, extreme pressures, temperatures over 450°C and acid chemicals, pose huge challenges for exploring craft.

375 Missions to Venus include Russia's Venera series (1961 to 1984), US Mariner probes (1962 to 1973) and *Pioneer Venus* (1978). From 1990 to 1994, *Magellan* used a radar to map the surface in amazing detail. In 2006, Europe's *Venus Express* began more mapping. Its instruments also studied Venus' extreme global warming.

◀ Studying Venus' atmosphere may help us understand similar climate processes happening on Earth.

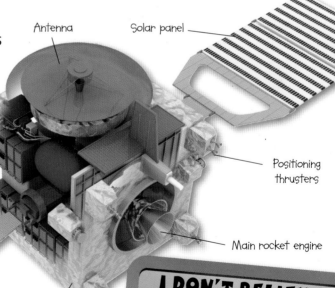

Antenna

Solar panel

Positioning thrusters

Main rocket engine

Gold coating helps to keep out the Sun's heat

▲ *Venus Express* orbits as low as 250 kilometres above the poles of Venus.

I DON'T BELIEVE IT!
The fastest spacecraft, and the fastest man–made object ever, was *Helios 2*. It neared the Sun at 67 kilometres per second!

Asteroids near and far

378 Asteroids orbit the Sun but are far smaller than planets, so even finding them is a challenge. Most large asteroids are in the main asteroid belt between Mars and Jupiter. Much closer to us are near-Earth Asteroids (NEAs), and more than 20 have been explored in detail by flyby craft, orbiters and landers.

Mars

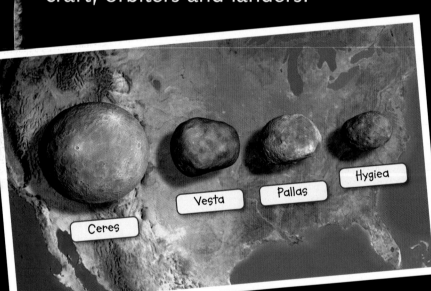

Ceres

Vesta

Pallas

Hygiea

379 Orbiting and landing on asteroids is very difficult. Many asteroids are oddly shaped, and they roll and tumble as they move through space. A craft may only discover this as it gets close.

◄ Dwarf planet Ceres and the three largest asteroids in our Solar System, seen against North America for scale. Vesta, the biggest asteroid, is about 530 kilometres across.

380 In 1996, the probe NEAR–Shoemaker launched towards NEA Eros. On the way it flew past asteroid Mathilde in the main belt. Then in 2000 it orbited 34-kilometre-long Eros, before landing. The probe discovered that the asteroid was peanut-shaped, and also gathered information about Eros' rocks, magnetism and movement. In 2008, spacecraft *Rosetta* passed main belt asteroid Steins, and asteroid Lutetia in 2010.

Jupiter

▲ In the main belt there are some dense 'asteroid swarms'. But most larger asteroids are tens of thousands of kilometres apart.

381 In 2010 Japan's *Hayabusa* brought back samples of asteroid Itokawa after touching down on its surface in 2005. This information has helped our understanding of asteroids as 'leftovers' from the formation of the Solar System 4600 million years ago.

382 *Dawn* was launched in 2007, to explore Vesta – the biggest asteroid – in 2011 and the dwarf planet Ceres in 2015. Vesta is rocky, while Ceres is thought to be icier, with various chemicals frozen as solids. *Dawn* aims to find out for sure.

▲ The *Dawn* mission badge shows its two main targets.

▶ *Hayabusa* was designed to gather samples of the asteroid Itokawa by firing a metal pellet towards the surface. It could then collect the dust thrown up by the impact.

Comet mysteries

383 Comets travel to and from the edges of the Solar System and beyond as they orbit the Sun. Unlike long-period comets, which may take thousands of years to orbit, short-period comets orbit every 200 years or less and so can be explored.

▶ The Oort cloud surrounds the Solar System and is made up of icy objects. It may be the source of some Sun-orbiting comets.

Sun

Kuiper belt

▶ The Kuiper belt lies beyond Neptune's orbit and is about twice the size of the Solar System. It consists of lots of comet-like objects.

Neptune

384 Like asteroids, comets are difficult to find. Comets warm up and glow only as they near the Sun. Their tails are millions of kilometres long, but consist only of faint gases and dust. The centre, or nucleus, of a comet may give off powerful jets of dust and gases that could blow a craft off course.

▶ A typical comet is mostly dust and ice. It has a glowing area, or coma, around it, and a long tail that points away from the Sun.

Solid rock core

Nucleus is often only a few kilometres across

Jets of gas and dust escape as ice melts

Glowing cloud, or coma, around nucleus is illuminated by sunlight

Dust and ice surrounds core

385 The famous Halley's Comet last appeared in 1986.

Several exploring craft, known as the 'Halley Armada', went to visit it. This included Europe's *Giotto* probe, which flew to within 600 kilometres of the comet's nucleus. There were also two Russian-French Vega probes, and *Sakigake* and *Suisei* from Japan.

▶ *Stardust* collected comet dust using a very lightweight foam, called aerogel, in a collector shaped like a tennis bat. The collector folded into the craft's bowl—like capsule for return to Earth.

386 In 2008, the *Stardust* probe returned a capsule of dust collected from the comet Wild 2.

In 2005, *Deep Impact* visited Comet Tempel 1 and released an impactor to crash into its nucleus and study the dust and gases given off. These craft increase our knowledge of comets as frozen balls of icy chemicals, rock and dust.

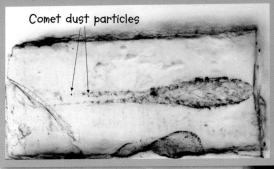

DUST COLLECTED FROM COMET WILD 2

Comet dust particles

▲ Under the microscope, a piece of *Stardust*'s aerogel (half the size of this 'o') is revealed to have minute dust particles embedded within it.

STARDUST APPROACHING COMET WILD 2

Glowing dust tail illuminated by sunlight

Ion (gas) tail appears bluish

SAMPLE CAPSULE RETURNS TO EARTH

Gas giants

387 The four furthest planets from Earth – Jupiter, Saturn, Uranus and Neptune – are 'gas giants'. These are large planets composed mainly of gases. It takes at least two years to reach Jupiter by the most direct route. But craft usually take longer because they use gravity assist.

▼ *Galileo* orbited Jupiter for more than seven years. It released an atmosphere probe to study the gases that make up almost the whole planet.

388 There have been seven flybys of Jupiter and each one discovered more of the planet's moons. The two US Voyager missions, launched in 1977, discovered that Jupiter has rings like Saturn. US spacecraft *Galileo* arrived in orbit around Jupiter in 1995 and released a probe into the planet's atmosphere.

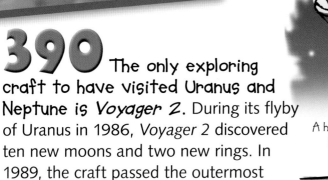

ON TITAN'S SURFACE

▲ *Huygens'* pictures from the surface of Titan, Saturn's largest moon, show lumps of ice and a haze of deadly methane gas.

389 The ringed planet Saturn had flybys by *Pioneer 11* (1979) and *Voyagers 1* and *2* (1980–1981). In 2004 the huge *Cassini-Huygens* craft arrived after a seven-year journey. The orbiter *Cassini* is still taking spectacular photographs of the planet, its rings and its moons.

▼ The *Huygens* lander separated from *Cassini* and headed for Titan. It sent back more than 750 images from the surface.

TITAN

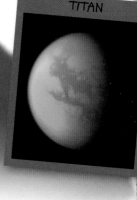

390 The only exploring craft to have visited Uranus and Neptune is *Voyager 2*. During its flyby of Uranus in 1986, *Voyager 2* discovered ten new moons and two new rings. In 1989, the craft passed the outermost planet, Neptune, and discovered six new moons and four new rings.

A heat shield prevented burn-up on entry

Parachutes slowed the lander's descent

Huygens lands on Titan

▼ The four gas giants have many moons — some large, and some very small. This list includes the five largest moons for each (not to scale).

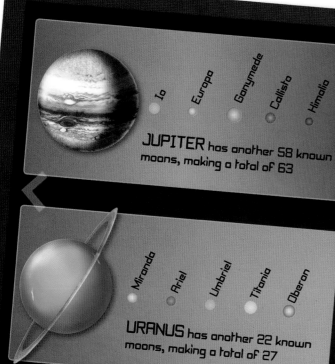

Io Europa Ganymede Callisto Himalia

JUPITER has another 58 known moons, making a total of 63

Miranda Ariel Umbriel Titania Oberon

URANUS has another 22 known moons, making a total of 27

Tethys Dione Rhea Titan Iapetus

SATURN has another 57 known moons, making a total of 62

Galatea Larissa Proteus Triton Nereid

NEPTUNE has another eight known moons, making a total of 13

Into the future

391 Sending craft to the edges of the Solar System takes many years. US spacecraft *New Horizons* was launched in 2006, and is now heading for dwarf planet Pluto. The craft is due to reach Pluto in 2015 and may continue into the Kuiper Belt, the home of comets and more dwarf planets.

392 *New Horizons'* immense nine-year journey was complicated to plan. It includes a flyby of tiny asteroid 132534 APL, then a swing around Jupiter for gravity assist and a speed boost. Flybys of Jupiter's moons are also planned, before the long cruise to tiny Pluto. Without Jupiter's gravity assist, the trip would be five years longer.

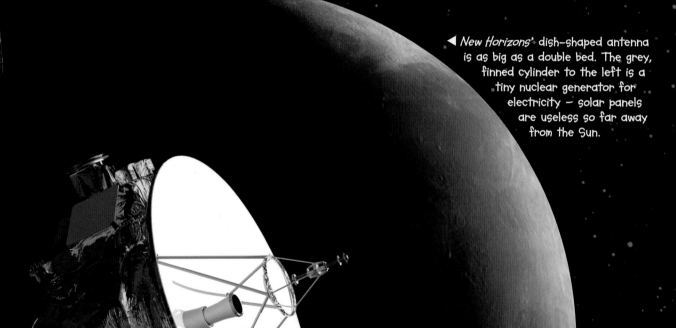

◄ *New Horizons'* dish-shaped antenna is as big as a double bed. The grey, finned cylinder to the left is a tiny nuclear generator for electricity — solar panels are useless so far away from the Sun.

393

Several major explorations are planned for the coming years. The *ExoMars* mission consists of a lander and a rover, due to launch in 2016 and 2018. They will look for signs of life on Mars, using a 2-metre-deep drill. The *BepiColombo* mission aims to orbit Mercury and measure the Sun's power.

◀ The *BepiColombo* mission is planned for launch in 2016. The six-year trip will take the craft past the Moon, Earth and Venus before reaching Mercury — the closest planet to the Sun.

394

What happens to exploring spacecraft? Some are deliberately crashed into other worlds, so that the impact can be observed by other spacecraft or from Earth. Others burn up as they enter the atmosphere of a planet or large moon.

▲ The drill on *ExoMars* rover will pass soil samples to the mini laboratory on board for analysis.

395

Many exploring spacecraft are still travelling in space, and will be for thousands of years. As they run out of power they become silent, either sitting on their target worlds or drifting though empty space – unless they crash into an object. The most distant craft is *Voyager 1*, launched in 1977. It is now more than 17 billion kilometres from Earth, and is still being tracked.

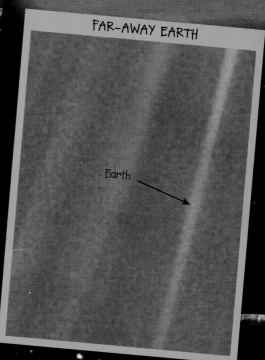

FAR-AWAY EARTH

Earth

▶ The 'Pale Blue Dot' photograph captured in 1990 by *Voyager 1*, was taken from six billion kilometres away. Earth is the tiny speck.

Space magic and myth

396 Exploring space has long been a favourite subject for story-telling. Even before rockets, there were theories about space travel and aliens. One of the first was *War of the Worlds*, written in 1898 by H G Wells.

▲ H G Wells' original story is brought to life in the 1953 movie *War of the Worlds*, in which martians invade Earth and destroy city after city. Humans can't stop them, but instead, germs eventually wipe out the alien invaders.

◄ The mission statement of *Star Trek*'s starship *Enterprise* was: 'To explore strange new worlds, to seek out new life and new civilizations, to boldly go where no one has gone before.'

397 In the 1950s, as humans began to explore space, tales of sightings of 'flying saucers' and UFOs (Unidentified Flying Objects) soared. Some of these may be explained by secret aircraft or spacecraft being tested by governments. A few people claimed that aliens visited Earth and left signs, such as strange patterns in fields called crop circles.

398 The *Star Wars* (1977 onwards) and *Alien* movies (1979–2007) are all about adventures in space. This genre grew in popularity at the same time that space exploration was becoming a reality. The *Star Trek* movies (1979 onwards) had several spin-off television series, including *Voyager* and *Deep Space Nine*.

399 In the future, scientists may discover a form of ultra-fast travel involving black holes and wormholes (tunnels through space and time). This could allow humans to travel to distant galaxies to look for other 'Goldilocks' planets similar to Earth. Like the third bowl of porridge in the nursery story, the conditions on a Goldilocks planet are not too hot and not too cold, but 'just right' for life to exist. As yet, no others have been discovered.

QUIZ

1. What was the name of the story written by H G Wells about an alien invasion of Earth?
2. What does UFO stand for?
3. What is a 'Goldilocks' planet?

Answers:
1. War of the Worlds
2. Unidentified Flying Object
3. A planet that has the perfect conditions for life to exist – not too hot, not too cold, but 'just right'

400 Space scientists have suggested new kinds of rockets and thrusters for faster space travel. These could reduce the journey time to the next-nearest star, Proxima Centauri, to about 100 years. But one day we may be beaten to it – aliens from a distant galaxy could be exploring space right now and discover us first!

▼ Virgin Galactic will soon be offering space travel to the general public. A ticket for a flight on SpaceShipTwo (below) will cost $200,000!

N339SS

SPACE TRAVEL

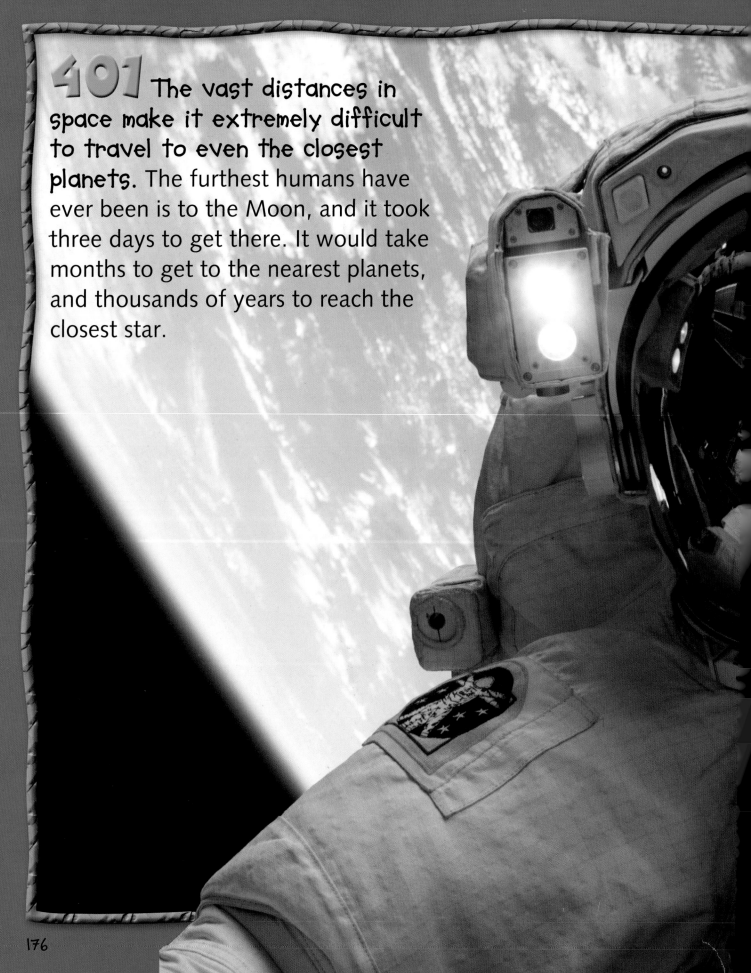

401 The vast distances in space make it extremely difficult to travel to even the closest planets. The furthest humans have ever been is to the Moon, and it took three days to get there. It would take months to get to the nearest planets, and thousands of years to reach the closest star.

◀ Astronauts can now live in space, in the orbiting International Space Station, seen here reflected in the visor of NASA astronaut Mike Hopkins' spacesuit.

Escape from Earth

402 Gravity is the force that pulls everything down towards Earth. All objects are pulled towards each other by gravity, but bigger things have a stronger pull. Earth is huge, and so pulls everything smaller towards it. This is why you don't float away, and why it is difficult to travel into space.

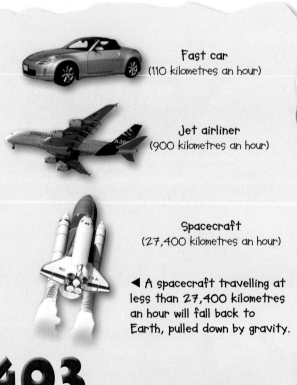

Fast car
(110 kilometres an hour)

Jet airliner
(900 kilometres an hour)

Spacecraft
(27,400 kilometres an hour)

◀ A spacecraft travelling at less than 27,400 kilometres an hour will fall back to Earth, pulled down by gravity.

403 The way to overcome this pull of gravity and reach space is to travel very fast. A spacecraft must get up to a speed of about 27,400 kilometres an hour. This is about 30 times faster than a cruising jet airliner, and 250 times faster than a car travelling on a motorway.

404 Even 27,400 kilometres an hour is not fast enough for a spacecraft to break free of Earth's gravity. At this speed it will circle round Earth about 200 kilometres above the ground – it is in orbit. Spacecraft orbit at different speeds depending on their distance from Earth – the pull of gravity decreases the further you are from Earth.

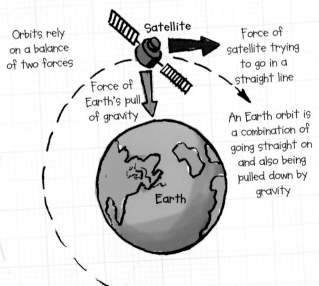

Orbits rely on a balance of two forces

Satellite

Force of satellite trying to go in a straight line

Force of Earth's pull of gravity

An Earth orbit is a combination of going straight on and also being pulled down by gravity

Earth

▲ Satellites orbiting closer to Earth must travel much faster than those in higher orbits.

▶ An Atlas rocket gave the *New Horizons* space probe the fastest ever launch speed for its journey to distant Pluto.

405 Spacecraft need even more speed to escape from the pull of Earth's gravity completely and fly off into space. They have to travel at 40,000 kilometres an hour – this speed is called Earth's escape velocity. Once in space there is no air to slow a spacecraft down, so it doesn't need powerful engines to keep going.

406 Distances in space are vast – so huge that astronomers do not use kilometres or miles to measure them. One measure of distance is the light-year, which is the distance that light travels in one year, and is equal to 9.46 million million kilometres. The nearest star to the Sun is 4.2 light-years away – equivalent to nearly 40 million million kilometres.

Sun

Light takes 8 minutes to reach Earth from the Sun

Earth

▲ A car travelling at 60 kilometres an hour would take 285 years to get to the Sun.

Rocket power

407 Rocket engines provide the enormous power needed to launch a spacecraft with enough speed to fly into space. On Earth, engines use oxygen from the air to burn their fuel, but in space there is no air to provide oxygen. Rocket engines can work in space because they have their own supply of oxygen gas.

408 Inside a rocket engine, fuel is burnt to make hot gases. The gases shoot out of a nozzle at the back of the rocket, pushing it forwards at high speed. Some rockets use a liquid fuel, which is pumped into the engine where it is mixed with oxygen and burnt. Other rockets use solid fuel – a rubbery material containing oxygen.

Key

① Satellite payload

② Second stage

③ First stage

④ Liquid oxygen tank

⑤ Liquid hydrogen fuel tank

⑥ Booster rocket

⑦ Solid fuel

⑧ First stage engine

▶ An Ariane 5 rocket has two stages and two solid rocket boosters to launch satellites into orbit.

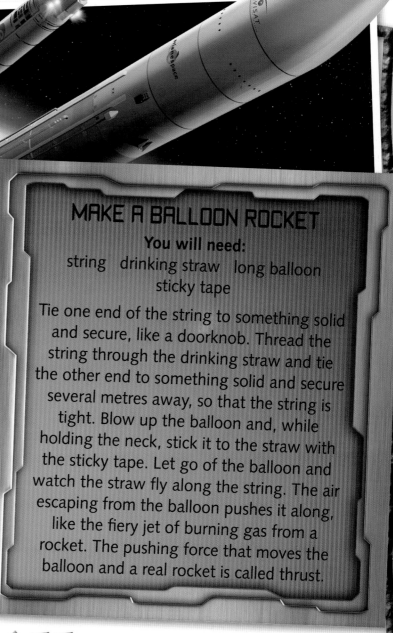

409
Booster rockets can supply extra power for a launch. These are separate rockets strapped to the side of the main rocket. They burn their fuel then break away and fall back to Earth. The space shuttle used two huge booster rockets, and the Russian Soyuz rockets have four boosters strapped around them at take-off.

▶ Ariane 5 boosters burn their fuel in about two minutes then fall away into the sea.

▲ Ariane 5 launch: Lift-off (1), boosters fall away (2), first stage separates (3), second stage puts satellite into orbit (4).

MAKE A BALLOON ROCKET
You will need:
string   drinking straw   long balloon
sticky tape

Tie one end of the string to something solid and secure, like a doorknob. Thread the string through the drinking straw and tie the other end to something solid and secure several metres away, so that the string is tight. Blow up the balloon and, while holding the neck, stick it to the straw with the sticky tape. Let go of the balloon and watch the straw fly along the string. The air escaping from the balloon pushes it along, like the fiery jet of burning gas from a rocket. The pushing force that moves the balloon and a real rocket is called thrust.

410
Several rocket stages are needed to reach space. Each stage has its own engine and fuel. The first stage lifts the rocket and spacecraft off the ground. When it has used up its fuel, it separates from the rest of the rocket and falls back to Earth. The next stage engine starts up, giving the rocket extra speed. It then falls away and the third stage takes the spacecraft into orbit.

411
New space planes are being designed that may make it easier and cheaper to fly into space. One is called *Skylon*. It will have engines that can use oxygen gas from the air until it reaches space. This means it will be lighter and need less power to take off because it will carry less oxygen. *Skylon* will take off and land on a runway and will be able to fly many times.

Space shuttle

412 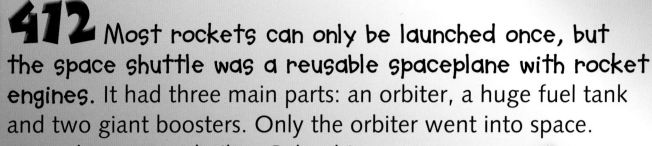 Most rockets can only be launched once, but the space shuttle was a reusable spaceplane with rocket engines. It had three main parts: an orbiter, a huge fuel tank and two giant boosters. Only the orbiter went into space. Five orbiters were built – *Columbia*, *Challenger*, *Discovery*, *Atlantis* and *Endeavour* – and each flew in space many times.

▶ At lift-off the enormous tank supplied the shuttle's three main engines with fuel. While the shuttle was attached to the tank during lift-off, its cargo bay doors were shut. The doors only opened when the shuttle reached orbit.

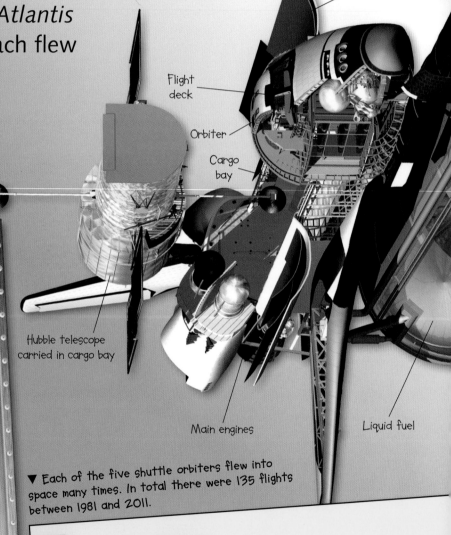

Cargo bay door

Flight deck

Orbiter

Cargo bay

Hubble telescope carried in cargo bay

Main engines

Liquid fuel

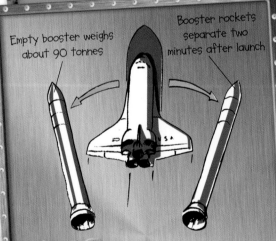

Empty booster weighs about 90 tonnes

Booster rockets separate two minutes after launch

413 The shuttle took off upwards like a rocket. The orbiter's three rocket engines and two huge booster rockets all fired together at launch. The solid fuel in the boosters only took two minutes to burn up, then they fell away into the sea.

▼ Each of the five shuttle orbiters flew into space many times. In total there were 135 flights between 1981 and 2011.

🚀 Shuttle flights

Orbiter	First flight	Last flight	No. of flights
Columbia	12 April, 1981	16 Jan, 2003	28
Challenger	4 April, 1983	28 Jan, 1986	10
Discovery	30 Aug, 1984	24 Feb, 2011	39
Atlantis	3 Oct, 1985	8 July, 2011	33
Endeavour	7 May, 1992	16 May, 2011	25

Fuel tank

Double-skin tank walls

Boosters

414 The shuttle orbiter could carry seven astronauts into space. They lived and worked in the cabin at the front of the orbiter on missions lasting one to two weeks at a time.

415 Satellites were launched from the shuttle's cargo bay. The shuttle placed the Hubble Space Telescope into orbit, and there were five later shuttle missions to repair it in space. On other flights the cargo bay held a laboratory called Spacelab where the astronauts carried out experiments.

416 The shuttle orbiters carried many of the International Space Station's parts into space. Space station modules where the astronauts would live and work fitted into the shuttle's cargo bay for the journey. Each part was added to the space station by spacewalking astronauts, who gradually built it while it orbited Earth.

▼ Space shuttle *Atlantis* docked with the ISS during the shuttle's final mission in July 2011.

Returning to Earth

417 One of the most dangerous parts of space travel is re-entry (returning to Earth's atmosphere). When spacecraft come back they rub against the air at incredible speeds, which makes them extremely hot. The space shuttle reached temperatures of about 1650°C on re-entry.

▲ The shuttle glowed red hot when re-entering Earth's atmosphere. To avoid burning up, spacecraft must re-enter at exactly the right angle.

418 Astronauts in a returning spacecraft are protected from the heat by a heat shield. On the space shuttle the heat shield was made of special tiles that covered the shuttle's underside. These stopped the heat from reaching the rest of the shuttle. Other spacecraft like the Russian Soyuz are protected by thick material that burns away but keeps the spacecraft cool.

419 The shuttle landed on a runway like an aircraft, but without using its engines, more like a huge glider. It travelled halfway round the world to its landing site, gliding through the air and slowing down by turning left and right. It came to a stop on the runway by using parachutes and brakes on its landing wheels to slow it. After servicing, the orbiter could be launched into space again.

▼ A Soyuz space capsule carrying three cosmonauts home from the *Mir* space station throws up dust as it lands in a desert area.

◄ The space shuttle needed a very long runway to land safely at the end of a mission.

420 The Soyuz spacecraft uses parachutes to slow it down as it falls through the air. Just before it hits the ground, small rocket motors fire to slow it even more and give it a soft landing. Some early spacecraft, like the Command Modules from the Apollo missions to the Moon, came down to Earth by parachute before splashing into the sea for a soft landing.

FEEL THE HEAT OF FRICTION

Rub your hands together or rub them against your legs. Do they start to feel warm? This is the way a spacecraft heats up when it rubs against the air. A force called friction makes the heat by trying to stop the rubbing movement. You can even start a fire using friction by rubbing two dry sticks together.

Spacecraft

421 Spacecraft are vehicles that travel to destinations in space. Some are built to carry people on board, but these do not travel far from Earth. Unmanned spacecraft can travel much further. People have sent unmanned spacecraft to all the other planets orbiting the Sun, and some space probes and rovers have even landed on some of them. Several have flown beyond the furthest planet in our Solar System, out towards the distant stars.

▶ The *Galileo* space probe orbited the giant planet Jupiter and dropped a smaller probe into Jupiter's bright clouds.

422 With no air to push against, a spacecraft will keep going steadily through space. However, spacecraft have engines to change direction and keep them on course, and to slow them down when they get to their destination. The engines can also provide extra speed to make the journey quicker. The spacecraft must carry all the fuel its engines need for the whole journey.

423 All spacecraft need power to operate and to keep warm – it is extremely cold in space. Solar panels that change sunlight into electricity can provide enough power for spacecraft close to the Sun. Those that travel far away from the Sun often use nuclear power. The space shuttle had fuel cells that made electricity by turning oxygen and hydrogen into water.

424 Spacecraft send back information and receive instructions from controllers on Earth using radio signals. As a spacecraft travels further away the radio signals get weaker. Probes going to distant planets need large dish-shaped antennae (aerials) to send and receive messages. Back on Earth, huge receivers collect the faint signals.

I DON'T BELIEVE IT!

UFOs (Unidentified Flying Objects) are objects in the sky that do not look like ordinary planes. Some people think that UFOs are alien spacecraft from other stars or planets visiting Earth, but there is no evidence for this.

425 Manned spacecraft must be able to keep the astronauts inside alive and well. They are built with a strong double outer layer to protect the crew from dangerous radiation and speeding space dust. They contain a supply of air to breathe and enough water and food for the whole journey. The temperature is kept comfortable using radiators to lose excess heat into space.

Astronauts

426 People who travel in space are called astronauts. In Russia they are called cosmonauts and in China they are called taikonauts. Astronauts from many different countries have gone into space, most of them in Russian and US spacecraft. So far, the only country other than Russia and the US to have launched astronauts into space is China.

▲ Trainee astronauts float inside an aircraft as if they are in space.

▶ ESA (European Space Agency) astronaut Jean-Francois Clervoy trains for spacewalks wearing a spacesuit underwater.

427 Astronauts need many months of training to get them ready for a spaceflight. They learn about the spacecraft they will be living and working in, and what to do in an emergency. Astronauts train in huge tanks of water to get used to the feeling of weightlessness and practise for spacewalks outside the spacecraft.

428
It is essential for astronauts to be fit and healthy. Before they fly there are many medical checks to make sure they will not fall ill in space. In their spacecraft they exercise regularly, usually for about two hours a day by using an exercise bike, running on a treadmill or doing a space version of weightlifting. This helps to keep their muscles and bones strong.

429
Living in space for a long time can make your muscles weaker and your body slightly taller. When floating in a spacecraft, you do not use the muscles that normally keep you standing up. The bones that make up your spine aren't squashed together by gravity, and so they stretch apart. Astronauts soon return to normal back on Earth.

430
Astronauts have many different jobs in space. Some are trained as pilots to fly the spacecraft. Others go outside the spacecraft or space station, where they carry out spacewalks to install equipment or do repairs. Inside, they perform experiments to explore the effects of space travel.

Key

1 Spine stretches, making astronauts taller

2 Leg and back muscles weaken

3 Leg and back bones get weaker and thinner

4 Face becomes puffy

▼ In space, gravity does not pull down on an astronaut's body.

Space pioneers

431 The first person to fly into space was a Russian called Yuri Gagarin. On 12 April, 1961 he completed one orbit round Earth in his spacecraft *Vostok 1*. Soon after Gagarin's flight, on 5 May, 1961, Alan Shepherd became the first American in space, although he didn't orbit Earth.

▲ Yuri Gagarin's historic flight lasted 1 hour and 48 minutes.

432 Two years after Gagarin's flight, on 16 June, 1963, Valentina Tereshkova became the first woman in space. She spent nearly three days in orbit, circling Earth 48 times during her flight in the *Vostok 6* spacecraft.

▲ Valentina Tereshkova was only 26 when she flew in space.

433 The first person to leave a spacecraft and go on a spacewalk was a Russian called Alexei Leonov, on 18 March, 1965. He was out in space for 12 minutes attached to his spacecraft by a tether to stop him floating away.

▲ Alexei Leonov left his *Voskhod* spacecraft through an airlock to perform the extremely dangerous spacewalk.

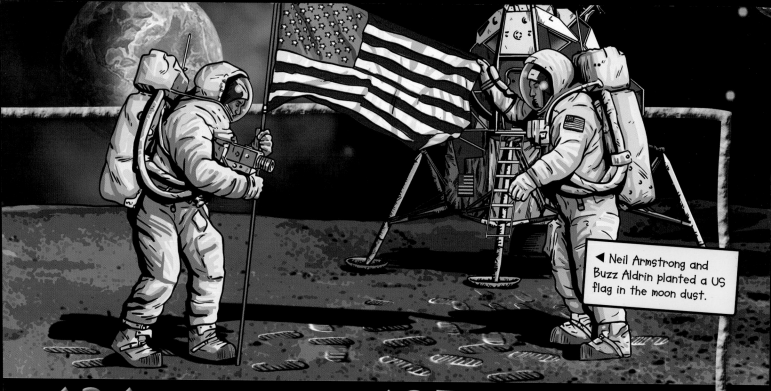

Neil Armstrong and Buzz Aldrin planted a US flag in the moon dust.

434 The first Moon landing took place on 20 July, 1969. Two American astronauts landed the *Apollo 11* lunar lander in an area of the Moon called the Sea of Tranquillity. Neil Armstrong was the first to set foot on the surface, followed by Buzz Aldrin. They spent about two and a half hours outside on the surface, exploring and collecting rocks to take back to Earth.

435 Since these early pioneers, several astronauts have spent over a year in space. Valeri Polyakov stayed aboard the *Mir* space station for nearly 438 days (about 14 months) in 1994 to 1995. Others have only spent longer in space if you add together all their different space flights. Sergei Krikalev has had six flights totalling over 800 days (over two years).

SPACE TIMELINE

4 October, 1957
The first artificial satellite, *Sputnik 1*, was launched.

3 November, 1957
A dog called Laika became the first animal in space.

12 April, 1961
The first human, Yuri Gagarin, was launched into space.

20 July, 1969
The first manned spacecraft landed on the Moon, and Neil Armstrong became the first person to walk on the surface.

18 March, 1965
Alexei Leonov was the first person to leave a spacecraft and 'walk' in space.

16 June, 1963
Valentina Tereshkova became the first woman in space.

19 April, 1971
The first space station, *Salyut 1*, was launched into orbit.

14 December, 1972
Apollo 17, the last manned mission to the Moon, left the Moon.

12 April, 1981
The first flight of the re-useable space shuttle.

20 February, 1986
The first module of the *Mir* space station was launched, with other modules and equipment added over the next 10 years.

31 October, 2000
The first crew visited the ISS.

20 November, 1998
The first module of the International Space Station (ISS), Zarya, was launched.

22 March, 1995
Valeri Polyakov set the record for the longest single spaceflight.

Spacesuits

436 Astronauts could not survive outside their spacecraft without a spacesuit. They put it on inside an airlock (airtight chamber) which has two doors, one opening into the spacecraft and the other to the outside. Once inside their suit they close the inner door, let the air out of the airlock, open the outer door and go outside.

437 Spacesuits are very bulky because they have to keep astronauts alive and protect them from speeding space dust. They are made of many different layers of material – 14 for a NASA spacesuit. The outer layers are waterproof, fireproof and bulletproof. Underneath are insulating layers that keep the temperature steady and a rip-proof layer that stops the suit from tearing.

438 The spacesuit must press down on an astronaut's body. Without this pressure their bodies would swell and gases would bubble out of their blood like boiling water. On Earth the air is always pressing down on our bodies, but in space there is no air. In a spacesuit the pressure comes from a double layer blown up like a balloon, in the shape of a human body.

Key

1. Lights
2. Helmet
3. Visor
4. Gloves
5. Control panel
6. Tether
7. Backpack with life support system
8. Boots

▲ Spacesuits provide a life-support system for astronauts while outside the spacecraft.

439 Astronauts wear special underwear under their spacesuits to keep them cool. The stretchy material fits closely, covering the whole body. Over 90 metres of thin tubing zig-zags through it. Cool water runs through these tubes, carrying heat away from the skin to the spacesuit backpack. Here the heat radiates out into space, cooling the water before it circulates through the tubes again.

440 Spacesuits have several different parts that all fit together with airtight seals. There are flexible joints in the shoulders, arms and wrists so that the astronauts can move their hands and arms to work in space. The helmet over the head is made of tough clear plastic to give the astronaut a good view. Under the helmet, a cap with a radio lets the astronaut talk to other astronauts or ground control.

I DON'T BELIEVE IT!

The NASA spacesuits that the astronauts wear on spacewalks at the ISS cost $12 million each. Astronauts do not have their own individual spacesuits. The parts come in different sizes so each astronaut can put together a spacesuit that fits him or her.

Spacewalks

441 Extravehicular Activity (EVA), often called a spacewalk, is when an astronaut leaves the spacecraft to work outside in space. They might be building or repairing a space station, or servicing satellites. Experiments that need to be exposed directly to space are fixed to the outside of a spacecraft and collected during spacewalks.

◄ This astronaut is working without a tether. He is wearing a SAFER (Simplified Aid for EVA Rescue) backpack. It can be controlled by small jets of nitrogen, which allow the astronaut to fly back to the space station.

442 A safety tether stops astronauts from floating away from their spacecraft. It is like a rope with one end fixed to the spacecraft and the other to the spacesuit. Tools used by the astronauts are also tethered to the spacesuit so they don't get lost in space.

I DON'T BELIEVE IT!
Spacewalking astronauts may have to stay in their spacesuits for up to eight hours without a toilet break. They wear a Maximum Absorption Garment (MAG) under their spacesuit to absorb the waste.

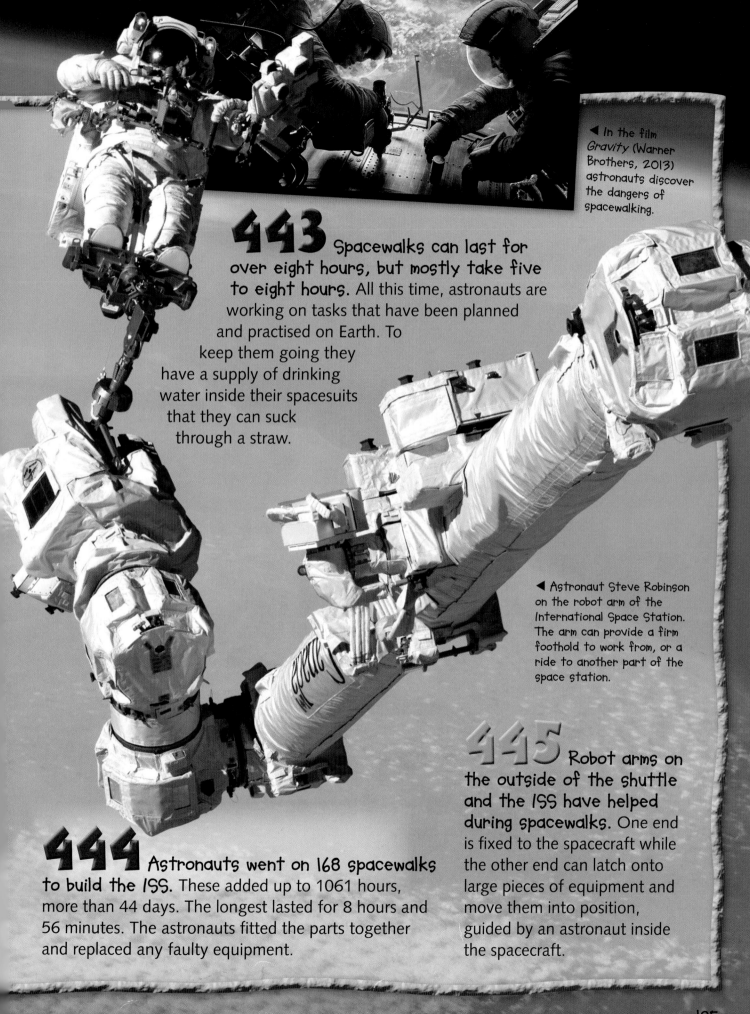

◀ In the film *Gravity* (Warner Brothers, 2013) astronauts discover the dangers of spacewalking.

443 Spacewalks can last for over eight hours, but mostly take five to eight hours. All this time, astronauts are working on tasks that have been planned and practised on Earth. To keep them going they have a supply of drinking water inside their spacesuits that they can suck through a straw.

◀ Astronaut Steve Robinson on the robot arm of the International Space Station. The arm can provide a firm foothold to work from, or a ride to another part of the space station.

445 Robot arms on the outside of the shuttle and the ISS have helped during spacewalks. One end is fixed to the spacecraft while the other end can latch onto large pieces of equipment and move them into position, guided by an astronaut inside the spacecraft.

444 Astronauts went on 168 spacewalks to build the ISS. These added up to 1061 hours, more than 44 days. The longest lasted for 8 hours and 56 minutes. The astronauts fitted the parts together and replaced any faulty equipment.

Living in space

446 The first thing you would notice on a spaceflight is that everything floats. This is called weightlessness. Spacecraft have footholds and straps to keep the astronauts in place while they are working or eating. Everything they use – notebooks, tools, cutlery, toiletries – must be fixed down or they would float away.

▼ Astronauts eating a meal from packets strapped to a table. They use spoons to eat the soft food.

447 All the food on the ISS is brought up from Earth. A lot is dried to save weight, even the drinks. There is no refrigerator so the food is sealed in packets or cans to stop it going off. The astronauts add water to the packet and shake before eating. They drink through a straw from a closed pack because liquids would float out of an open cup.

▼ 1. Wetting hair with drops of water.

▼ 2. Rubbing shampoo through hair.

▲ 3. Combing out clean hair.

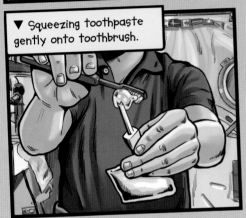

▼ Squeezing toothpaste gently onto toothbrush.

448 The ISS has no shower. Astronauts keep clean by washing with a soapy flannel. There is a limited supply of water because it must all be brought up from Earth, so they wash their hair with a special shampoo that doesn't need to be rinsed out. They also have edible toothpaste that they can swallow after brushing their teeth to avoid rinsing and spitting.

449 When astronauts sleep they must strap themselves down so they don't float around and bump into things. They usually sleep in sleeping bags fixed to a wall. There are small cabins in the ISS with just enough room for one astronaut in a sleeping bag. Some astronauts use sleep masks and earplugs to block out the noise and light.

▶ Many astronauts find it difficult to sleep soundly in space.

▼ Astronauts fasten themselves on to the toilet so they don't float off.

450 You cannot flush a toilet with water in space. Instead, air is used to suck the waste away from the astronauts' bodies. Urine is collected through a tube and cleaned, then the clean water is used again for drinking. All the water on the ISS is cleaned and recycled. The air is recirculated, removing the carbon dioxide breathed out by the astronauts and adding fresh oxygen.

Space stations

451 A space station provides a home in space where astronauts can live and work for months at a time. So far, space stations have all orbited Earth just a few hundred kilometres above its surface. The first space station to be launched was the Russian *Salyut 1* in 1971.

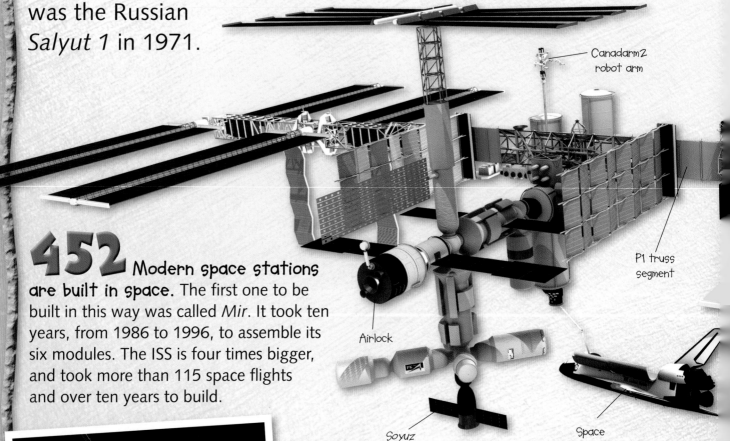

▼ The first module of the ISS was launched in 1998. Astronauts from 14 different countries have stayed in it since.

Canadarm2 robot arm

P1 truss segment

Airlock

Soyuz

Space Shuttle

452 Modern space stations are built in space. The first one to be built in this way was called *Mir*. It took ten years, from 1986 to 1996, to assemble its six modules. The ISS is four times bigger, and took more than 115 space flights and over ten years to build.

▲ The US Space Shuttle *Atlantis* docked with the Russian *Mir* space station in July 1995.

453 The ISS is over 100 metres long, about the length of an American football field. The space occupied by the astronauts is as big as a five bedroomed house, and has two bathrooms and a gym. It weighs about 450,000 kilograms – as much as 320 cars. Six astronauts make up a full crew. There have been people living on board the ISS since November 2000.

454

The electricity to run the ISS comes from the Sun. Eight huge pairs of solar panels, covered with solar cells, change sunlight into electricity. Each pair is about 35 metres long and 11.6 metres wide. Two panels end to end would stretch the width of an American football field. Altogether they make the 75 to 90 kilowatts of power needed to keep the ISS running. The panels twist round to face the Sun so they can make more electricity.

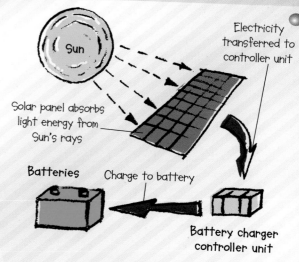

Sun

Electricity transferred to controller unit

Solar panel absorbs light energy from Sun's rays

Batteries

Charge to battery

Battery charger controller unit

▲ Batteries provide power when the ISS is in the Earth's shadow.

Solar panels

Main truss

455

The basic structure of the ISS is a long beam called a truss that holds the parts together. Attached to it are modules where the astronauts live and work, linked together by nodes. There are docking ports where visiting spacecraft lock on. This is also where supplies are unloaded and astronauts enter.

SPOT THE ISS

The ISS orbits Earth every 90 minutes, and can often be seen in a clear sky just before dawn or just after sunset. It looks like a bright star moving slowly across the sky. The website spotthestation.nasa. gov/sightings will tell you when and where to see it. Enter your country and city to find dates, times, which direction and how high to look in the sky.

456

Astronauts currently travel to and from the space station in a Russian Soyuz spacecraft. Supplies are also brought up to the space station on regular ferries without crews. Russia, Europe and Japan, as well as two private companies, have all launched unmanned supply spacecraft to the ISS.

Space tourists

457 A few very rich people have already paid for a trip into space. The first space tourist was an American called Dennis Tito, who flew to the International Space Station in a Soyuz spacecraft in 2001. His trip lasted for 8 days and cost $20 million.

▲ Cosmonaut Talgat Musabayev (right) helps Dennis Tito get used to weightlessness on his trip to the ISS.

458 Several private companies are now building space planes to take people on short flights into space. *SpaceShipTwo* is one space plane now being tested. It will not go into orbit, but will take six passengers into space for a short time before returning them to Earth.

▼ *SpaceShipTwo* is launched by a special aircraft called *White Knight Two*, which carries it to a height of 15 kilometres above Earth.

▼ The cost of a stay in a future space hotel would be enormous — millions of dollars.

459 In the future, space hotels could be built in orbit. These would be similar to a space station, but for visiting tourists instead of working astronauts. One company called Bigelow Aerospace has already launched inflatable spacecraft that could be built into a hotel, but none that people could live in.

▼ A space station from the science fiction film *Elysium* (TriStar Pictures, 2013).

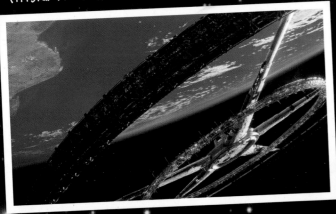

460 Other companies have suggested offering private space flights to land on the Moon, but one trip would cost billions of dollars. A cheaper option would be to fly in a huge loop around the Moon and back to Earth without landing. The passengers would get a close-up view of the Moon's surface, and would see the far side that cannot be seen from Earth.

I DON'T BELIEVE IT!
One space tourist has paid for two trips to the ISS. In 2007 Charles Simonyi spent 15 days in space, and enjoyed it so much he paid for a second visit in 2009, for another 14 days.

Journey to the Moon

461 Only twelve people have ever set foot on the Moon, and it all happened over 40 years ago. Six Apollo missions landed astronauts on the Moon over three years. The first was *Apollo 11* in July 1969 and the last was *Apollo 17* in December 1972.

▲ A Saturn V rocket launches the Apollo Command Module with three astronauts inside on their journey to the Moon.

462 The Saturn V rocket launched the Apollo spacecraft towards the Moon. It was the most powerful rocket ever to fly successfully. When it was full of fuel, ready for lift-off, it weighed 2.8 million kilograms – about as much as 400 elephants. It had three stages and was 111 metres tall – about as high as a 36-storey building.

463 The journey to the Moon took three days. Three astronauts travelled inside the Apollo Command Module. It was just big enough for the astronauts to move around, with about as much room inside as an estate car. It was perched on top of the Saturn V rocket for lift-off with the Lunar Module, which the astronauts later used to land on the surface.

▼ After the spacecraft was released from the rocket, the Command and Service Module docked with the Lunar Module for the journey to the Moon.

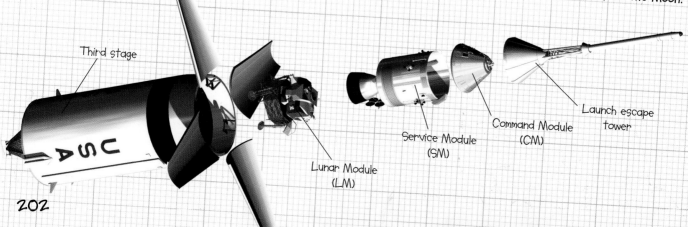

Third stage

Lunar Module (LM)

Service Module (SM)

Command Module (CM)

Launch escape tower

464 When they arrived, two of the astronauts entered the Lunar Module, which then flew down to land on the surface. The third astronaut stayed in the Command Module orbiting the Moon. At the end of the mission, the Lunar Module took off and docked with the Command Module. The astronauts travelled back in the Command Module, leaving the Lunar Module to crash into the Moon.

▶ The Apollo Lunar Module used its engine to land gently on the Moon.

I DON'T BELIEVE IT!

When the first astronauts returned to Earth from the Moon, they had to stay in quarantine for three weeks in case they had brought back any dangerous bugs that could affect people on Earth.

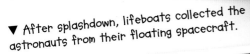
▼ After splashdown, lifeboats collected the astronauts from their floating spacecraft.

465 When it reached Earth, the Command Module with the astronauts inside flew back into the atmosphere. Large parachutes opened to slow it down as it fell towards the ground. It splashed down in the sea for a soft landing. Helicopters transported the astronauts and their spacecraft to a waiting recovery ship. They were then carried safely to land.

Exploring the Moon

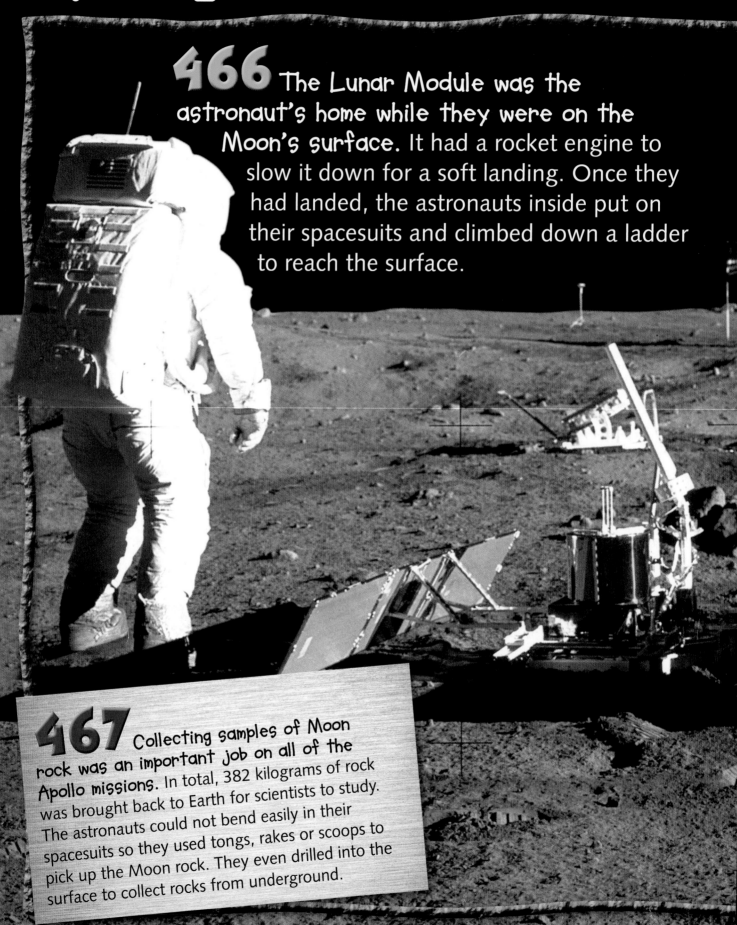

466 The Lunar Module was the astronaut's home while they were on the Moon's surface. It had a rocket engine to slow it down for a soft landing. Once they had landed, the astronauts inside put on their spacesuits and climbed down a ladder to reach the surface.

467 Collecting samples of Moon rock was an important job on all of the Apollo missions. In total, 382 kilograms of rock was brought back to Earth for scientists to study. The astronauts could not bend easily in their spacesuits so they used tongs, rakes or scoops to pick up the Moon rock. They even drilled into the surface to collect rocks from underground.

▶ Buzz Aldrin sets up experiments near the Lunar Module during the *Apollo 11* mission.

469 On the Moon the astronauts had to wear very bulky spacesuits for protection. On Earth these were very heavy, weighing 82 kilograms, similar to carrying another person around. But on the Moon the pull of gravity is much lower, and so they only weighed 14 kilograms.

470 On the last three Apollo missions, the astronauts had a lunar rover. This was an electric four-wheeled buggy about the size of a small car. It had two seats and room to carry Moon rock back to base. The astronauts used a joystick to drive it. The rover's maximum speed was only around 18 kilometres an hour, but it let the astronauts explore much further.

468 Each of the Apollo missions left experiments on the Moon. These included a mirror, used to bounce a beam of laser light back to Earth to accurately measure the distance. Others listened for moon quakes and monitored radiation. All the information was sent back to Earth as radio signals. Some of the experiments still work today.

HOW MUCH WOULD YOU WEIGH ON THE MOON?

You will need:
a set of bathroom scales

Weigh yourself on the scales and make a note of your weight. Divide it by six. This is what you would weigh on the Moon. Find something that weighs this amount when you put it on the scales – that's how light you would feel on the Moon.

Satellites at work

471 As well as the ISS, hundreds of satellites constantly orbit Earth. Many are in an orbit called geostationary orbit, 35,786 kilometres above Earth. These circle at the same rate as Earth spins. This means that they stay above the same point on Earth, so aerials on the ground do not have to move to catch their signals.

▲ Over half a million pieces of space junk also orbit Earth, making space travel even more dangerous.

Solar panels turn to face Sun

Solar panels provide power

◄ Aerials on *Intelsat* communications satellites relay radio signals from one part of the world to another.

Satellite points down to Earth

Aerials send and receive radio signals

472 Communications satellites send radio signals carrying telephone conversations and TV programmes all around the world. Pictures of news and events from distant countries travel up to a satellite in space then back down to Earth to get to your TV. Satellites also let us talk on the phone to people thousands of miles away.

QUIZ

1. What kind of signals do communications satellites send?
2. How high above Earth is geostationary orbit?
3. Which kind of satellite watches cloud movements and measures temperatures?

Answers:
1. Radio signals
2. 35,786 kilometres
3. A meteorological or weather satellite

473 Navigation satellites can tell you where you are, how fast you are moving and direct you to where you are going. The Global Positioning System (GPS) has around 30 satellites circling Earth. Satnav equipment picks up signals from several satellites and uses the information to work out your position and speed.

▶ Each *Navstar* navigation satellite circles Earth twice every day, so that signals from at least four satellites are available everywhere on Earth.

474 Meteorological satellites help forecasters predict the weather. They look at Earth's atmosphere, watching cloud movements and measuring land and sea temperatures. The information is sent to huge computers, which use it to calculate weather forecasts.

▼ *Solar and Heliospheric Observatory (SOHO)* orbits between Earth and the Sun to give early warning of Sun storms.

475 Satellites looking down from space can spot pollution on Earth. They can also track wild animals and icebergs, and spot forest fires. Astronomical satellites look out into space to discover planets around distant stars, and find out what the Universe was like billions of years ago. Some watch the Sun for storms that could send dangerous bursts of radiation towards Earth.

Long distance space travel

476 A journey through space must be planned very carefully. Everything in space is moving very fast, so when launching a spacecraft mission planners have to decide which way to send it to make sure it doesn't miss its target.

▲ Voyager 2 captured close up pictures of the planet Neptune as it flew past in 1989.

▶ When *Voyager 2* flew by Jupiter in 1979 it used the giant planet's gravity to pick up speed and change direction for its rendezvous with Saturn.

Jupiter

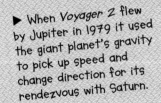
Voyager 2

477 Spacecraft can save fuel on a journey by swinging around a planet to gain speed. This is called a sling shot or gravity assist, because it uses the gravity of the planet to propel it on its way much faster. The Voyager 2 space probe flew past the four furthest planets from the Sun – Jupiter, Saturn, Uranus and Neptune. At each of these it gained enough speed to reach the next.

I DON'T BELIEVE IT!

Launched in 1977, the *Voyager 1* space probe has now reached the edge of the Solar System – about 19 billion kilometres away. It is still sending back information, but its signals take over 16 hours to reach Earth.

478 Ion engines can gradually provide extra speed over the vast distances in space. They use magnets to send a stream of tiny electrical particles called ions out of the engine, pushing the spacecraft forwards. They only provide a very tiny thrust (push) but they can keep going, unlike rocket engines, which run out of fuel. In the future, they may help spacecraft reach the outer Solar System.

◄ The *SMART-1* spacecraft used ion engines on its flight to the Moon in 2003.

479 Solar sails may also be used to push spacecraft along in the future. They are huge sheets of very thin, light material that are pushed along by sunlight. Spacecraft with solar sails would be launched by a rocket, then the sail would unfold. The sunlight gives a weak but constant push to the sail, which gradually gains speed. In 2010 Japan launched the first solar sailing spacecraft called *IKAROS*.

▼ In the future, huge solar sails like this could propel spacecraft through space.

480 Radio signals take a long time to travel to and from spacecraft far out in space. When controllers on Earth send instructions to a spacecraft exploring Mars, they may arrive up to 20 minutes later. This is much too late to stop a rover colliding with a rock, so many spacecraft are programmed to operate without instructions from Earth.

Robot travellers

481 Space probes are unmanned craft that travel through space to explore planets, moons, asteroids and comets. Probes have investigated all the planets in our Solar System. They carry instruments and cameras to measure temperatures, radiation and magnetism.

I DON'T BELIEVE IT!

Aerogel is an extremely light material, mostly made up of empty space. In 2004 the *Stardust* probe used aerogel to collect particles of comet dust as it could trap the tiny particles without damaging them.

▼ After a seven year journey to Saturn the *Cassini* probe dropped a smaller probe onto Saturn's moon Titan.

482 Some probes fly close to their target but do not stop. They collect pictures and information, then fly on. Others go into orbit around it. They can send back pictures of the whole surface and watch for changes. For a really close look, some spacecraft actually land on their target. They can find out what the surface is made of around their landing site.

▼ The *Curiosity* rover moves very slowly, covering only about 30 metres in an hour.

483 The *Curiosity* rover is a robot spacecraft that is currently exploring the planet Mars. It is a six-wheeled rover about the size of a car that moves slowly across the dusty surface, steering to avoid any large rocks. It takes close-up pictures of the soil and rocks, and can drill into the rocks and test them to see what they are made of.

484 Several space probes have been sent out to intercept comets. *Giotto* was the first probe to send back pictures of a comet's nucleus, which cannot be seen from Earth. It photographed Halley's comet in 1986. The *Stardust* probe collected tiny dust particles from comet Wild 2's huge glowing tail in 2004. It flew back to Earth and delivered a capsule containing the samples, before continuing on to begin a new mission.

485 Asteroids (chunks of rock that orbit the Sun between the planets Mars and Jupiter) are also a target for space probes. *Hayabusa* is a Japanese probe that landed on a small asteroid called Itokawa in 2005. It brought a sample of asteroid dust back to Earth for scientists to study.

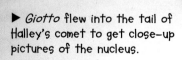
▶ *Giotto* flew into the tail of Halley's comet to get close-up pictures of the nucleus.

▲ The nucleus of Halley's comet was tiny and very dark.

A visit to Mars?

486 The next possible place for astronauts to visit is Mars. There have been plans to send people to Mars even before the first Moon landing, although it would be a very dangerous and expensive mission. People could not survive on Mars without spacesuits and they would need protection from radiation and the extreme cold.

▶ Astronauts on a visit to Mars could use a rover to explore Mars' rocky surface and as a base to live in.

Astronauts might not wear spacesuits inside the rover

487 It would take six to nine months to travel to Mars, and the same for the trip back. One mission that has been suggested would fly two people to Mars, not to land, but to go around it and back to Earth. The trip would take nearly 17 months, and the crew would spend all of this time inside their spacecraft. If astronauts landed on Mars, they could be away from Earth for two years or more.

QUIZ
1. Is there water on Mars?
2. How long would a round trip to Mars take?
3. Could astronauts breathe the air on Mars?

Answers:
1. Yes, but it is frozen 2. 17 months if you did not stop and land on Mars 3. No, the air on Mars does not contain oxygen

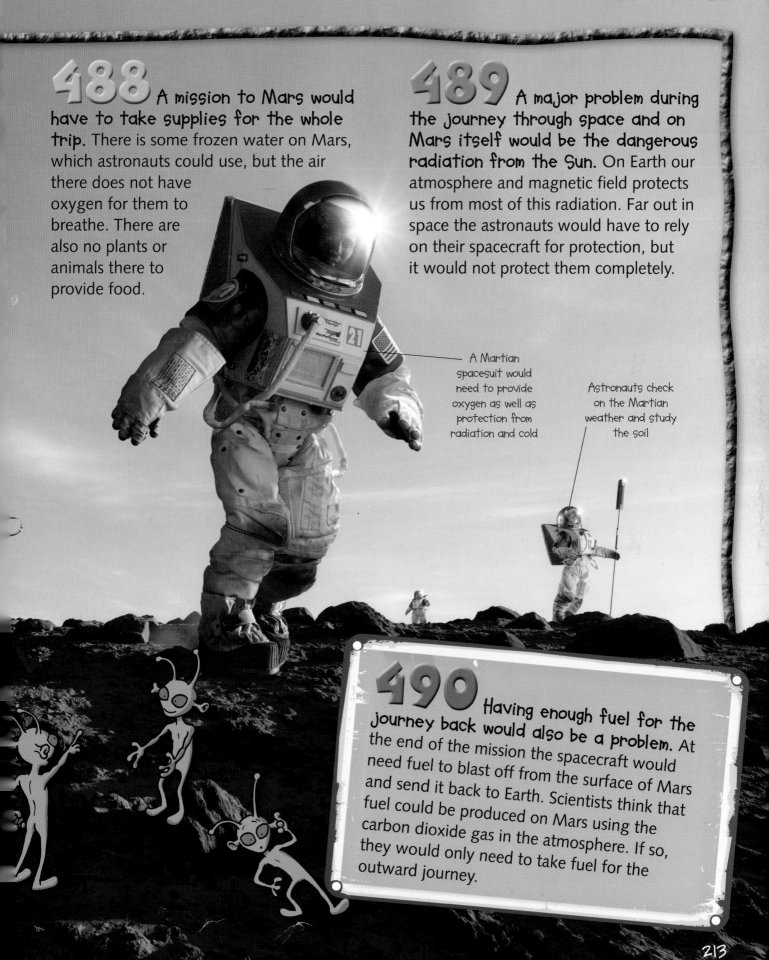

488 A mission to Mars would have to take supplies for the whole trip. There is some frozen water on Mars, which astronauts could use, but the air there does not have oxygen for them to breathe. There are also no plants or animals there to provide food.

489 A major problem during the journey through space and on Mars itself would be the dangerous radiation from the Sun. On Earth our atmosphere and magnetic field protects us from most of this radiation. Far out in space the astronauts would have to rely on their spacecraft for protection, but it would not protect them completely.

A Martian spacesuit would need to provide oxygen as well as protection from radiation and cold

Astronauts check on the Martian weather and study the soil

490 Having enough fuel for the journey back would also be a problem. At the end of the mission the spacecraft would need fuel to blast off from the surface of Mars and send it back to Earth. Scientists think that fuel could be produced on Mars using the carbon dioxide gas in the atmosphere. If so, they would only need to take fuel for the outward journey.

Starships

491 People will not be able to travel to distant stars any time soon. This is because of the huge distances between stars and the time it would take. Maybe in the future starships will be built in orbit around the Earth, using materials mined on the Moon, and sent out to explore the Universe.

▼ A starship finds a distant planet but would humans be able to live there?

I DON'T BELIEVE IT!

NASA and America's Defense Advanced Research Projects Agency (DARPA) have started a project to look at the possibility of star travel. They expect it will take 100 years to solve the problems of travelling to other stars.

492 The biggest problem with starship travel is the enormous distances in space. Nothing travels faster than light but even light takes over four years to reach the nearest star. The spacecraft humans have built so far can only manage a tiny fraction of this speed and even the fastest would take thousands of years to get there.

493 People have suggested that the human crew of a starship could go into hibernation for the journey by lowering their temperature to below freezing. However, we do not know if they would survive and wake up at the end of the journey. Some frogs and tiny microscopic creatures can survive being frozen but it has not been tried with humans.

▲ If a human space crew was put into 'hibernation' for a journey to a distant star, computers would pilot the starship and revive them after the long journey.

494 A huge starship that is completely self-sufficient is called an 'interstellar ark'. It would be big enough to grow food for everyone on board and recycle the air and water, just like an island in space. It would spin slowly to give the crew the feeling of gravity. People would live their whole lives and have children and grandchildren during the voyage. Eventually the descendants of the original crew would arrive at their destination.

▼ In the film *Avatar* (20th Century Fox, 2009), the aliens are 3 metres tall and have blue skin.

495 Nobody knows what these space travellers would find if they reached another world. They would hope to find another planet like Earth where they could live. However, other planets may not have the water and oxygen that humans need to survive. If they did find a planet that humans could live on it might already have inhabitants who would not welcome a starship full of people, all of whom would seem like aliens to them.

Space travel in books and films

496 Travelling through space to distant stars and galaxies is a common theme in science fiction. Before rockets were invented, authors imagined materials and technology that could overcome gravity and send people into space. In his 1865 story, *From the Earth to the Moon*, Jules Verne used a giant cannon to shoot space travellers to the Moon.

▶ The starship *Enterprise* in *Star Trek* had 'warp drive' — a propulsion system that allowed it to travel faster than light.

497 Stories would not be very exciting if spaceships took thousands of years to travel between stars. Instead, authors invent special devices to allow them to travel faster than light. Films like *Star Wars* use 'Hyperspace' — highways through space where spaceships can travel faster than light.

498 Weightlessness is not always a problem for astronauts in films. They walk around in their spaceships as though on Earth. Starships in films are also very spacious inside with plenty of room for astronauts to move about. It looks very different from the way the real astronauts live on the International Space Station.

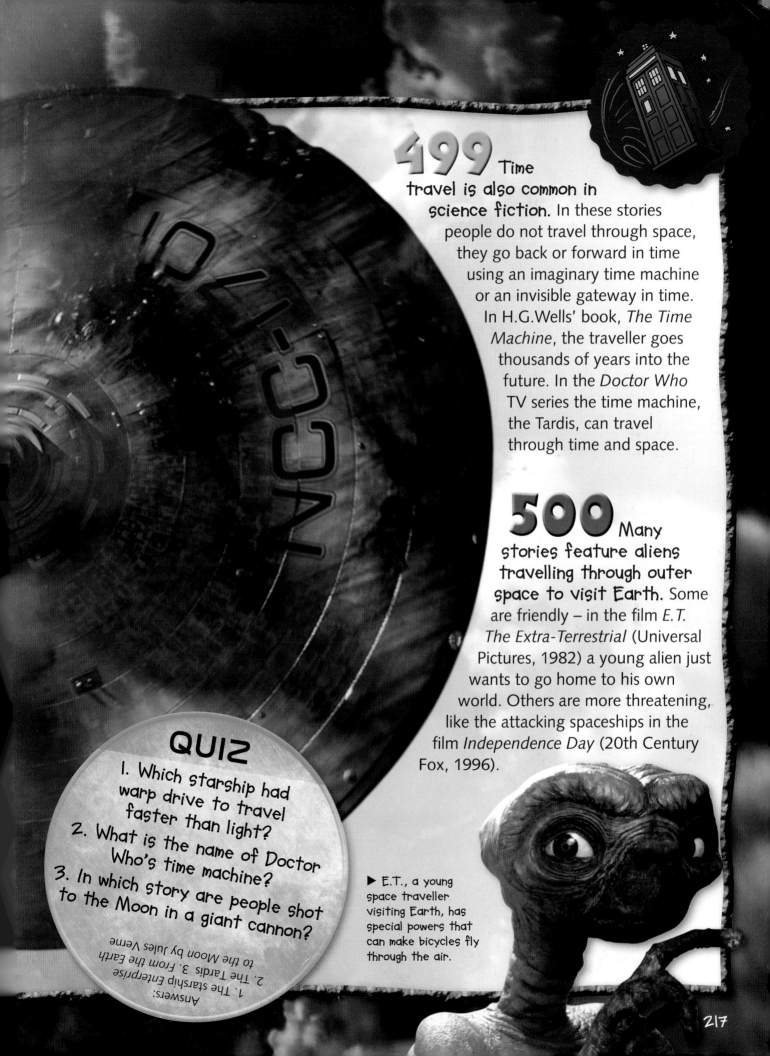

499 Time travel is also common in science fiction. In these stories people do not travel through space, they go back or forward in time using an imaginary time machine or an invisible gateway in time. In H.G.Wells' book, *The Time Machine*, the traveller goes thousands of years into the future. In the *Doctor Who* TV series the time machine, the Tardis, can travel through time and space.

500 Many stories feature aliens travelling through outer space to visit Earth. Some are friendly – in the film *E.T. The Extra-Terrestrial* (Universal Pictures, 1982) a young alien just wants to go home to his own world. Others are more threatening, like the attacking spaceships in the film *Independence Day* (20th Century Fox, 1996).

▶ E.T., a young space traveller visiting Earth, has special powers that can make bicycles fly through the air.

QUIZ

1. Which starship had warp drive to travel faster than light?
2. What is the name of Doctor Who's time machine?
3. In which story are people shot to the Moon in a giant cannon?

Answers:
1. The starship Enterprise
2. The Tardis 3. From the Earth to the Moon by Jules Verne

217

INDEX

ACKNOWLEDGEMENTS

The publishers would like to thank the following sources for the use of their photographs:
t = top, b = bottom, l = left, r = right, c = centre, bg = background, m = main, rt = repeated throughout

Cover: *Front* (t) Detlev van Ravenswaay/NASA/Science Photo Library, (b) Geo Images/Alamy; *Spine* GReat Images in NASA (NASA-GRIN); *Back* (c) NASA/JPL-Caltech, (l) NASA/JPL-Caltech, (r) NASA, ESA, and the Hubble Heritage Team (STScI/AURA)-ESA/Hubble Collaboration

Alamy 12(m) NG Images; 32(tr) Galaxy Picture Library; 157(tr) Keith Morris

ALMA 87(b) (ESO/NAOJ/NRAO), C.Padilla

Corbis 24(b) YONHAP/epa; 29(tr) Caren Brinkema/Science Faction; 36(b) NASA – JPL, (cr) NASA; 43(tr); 82(tr) Blue Lantern Studio; 84–85(bg) Stapleton Collection; 101(c) Araldo de Luca; 115(tl) IAC/GTC; 143 Roger Ressmeye; 153(t) Michael Benson/Kinetikon Pictures; 162(t) Bill Ingalls/NASA/Handout/CNP; 163(t) Roger Ressmeyer; 179(m) Scott Andrews/Science Faction; 185(tr) Alexander Nemenov/epa; 186–187(m) Roger Ressmeyer; 201(r) and 209(b) Victor Habbick Visions/Science Photo Library

Dreamstime 110(c) Kramer-1; 118(t) Silverstore

European Space Agency (ESA) 6(cr) D. Ducros; 15(br) ESA-Anneke Le Floc'h; 27(bl) ESA/ÖWF/P. Santek; 37(br) NASA/JPL/Space Science Institute; 54(tr) ESA/Hubble & NASA, Judy Schmidt; 55(tr) ESA–D.Ducros, 2013, (cl) ESA/Hubble & NASA; 57(tr) NASA, ESA & Hubble Heritage Team (AURA/STScI), (br) J.P. Harrington (University of Maryland) and K.J. Borkowski (NCSU) and NASA; 63(bl) NASA, ESA and H. Bond (STScI); 66–67(bg) ESA Adrienne Cool (SFSU) et al., Hubble Heritage Team (STScI/AURA), NASA; 71(c) NASA/ESA/J.Hester and A.Loll (Arizona State Univ.); 72(c) NASA/Dana Berry; 76(c) NASA, ESA, and the Hubble Heritage Team (STScI/AURA)-ESA/Hubble Collaboration; 77(b) ESA/Herschel/PACS/MESS Key Programme Supernova Remnant Team, NASA, ESA and Allison Loll/Jeff Hester (Arizona State University); 88(c) ESA/NASA/Geneva University Observatory(Frederic Pont); 146(r) D. Ducros; 161 Mars Express D. Ducros; 162–163(b); 165(bl) 2007 MPS/DLR-PF/IDA; 171(tl) ESA/NASA/JPL/University of Arizona; 173(t) C. Carreau, (tr) AOES Medialab

Fotolia.com 96(l) Sharpshot; 107(tl) Georgios Kollidas, (r) Konstantin Sutyagin; 110(tc) pdtnc; 110–111(bg) Jenny Solomon; 130(clockwise from bl) Stephen Coburn, Petar Ishmeriev, pelvidge, Mats Tooming; 136(bl) D.aniel

Getty 159(br) Time & Life Pictures; 158–159(bg) SSPL via Getty Images; 170 Time & Life Pictures

Glow Images 26(t) SuperStock, (cr) Stocktrek Images/Walter Myers; 33(m) Stocktrek Images/Ron Miller; 38 (m) Sciepro/Science Photo Library

iStockphoto.com 56(bl) duncan1890; 106–107(bg) Duncan Walker; 107(br) Steven Wynn; 108(cr) Steven Wynn; 109(br) Steven Wynn; 110(tl) HultonArchive; 111(tc) Duncan Walker; 142–143(bg) Nicholas Belton; 150(r) Jan Rysavy

NASA 2–3; 5(tl) NASA/JPL-Caltech, (cr) NASA/JPL-Caltech, (br) NASA CXC/NGST; 6(tl); 10(b) MPIA/NASA/Calar Alto Observatory, (t) NASA, C.R.O; 15(cl), (bl); 19(b); 26(c) NASA/JPL; 27(timeline, tl) NASA/JPL-Caltech, (timeline, tr) NASA/JPL-Caltech, (timeline, bl) NASA/JPL-Caltech/MSSS, (timeline, br) NASA/JPL-Caltech/MSSS; 28(br) NASA/JPL; 29(bl) NASA/JPL/JHUAPL; 32(bl); 35(tr) NASA/JPL-Caltech/SSI; 37(bl) ESA/NASA/JPL/University of Arizona, (c) NASA/JPL/Space Science Institute, (cr) Cassini Imaging Team, SSI, JPL, ESA, NASA; 38(br) NASA/JPL; 39(bl) NASA/JPL/USGS, (bc), (br); 40(br) Voyager 2, NASA; 41(t) Voyager Project, JPL, NASA, (br) Voyager 2, NASA; 46(bl) GReat Images in NASA (NASA-GRIN), (br) NASA/JPL-Caltech/Malin Space Science Systems; 49(tl) Debra Meloy Elmegreen (Vassar College) et al., & the Hubble Heritage Team (AURA/STScI/NASA), (bl) NASA, ESA, K. Noll (STScI); 56(c) Subaru Telescope (NAOJ), Hubble Space Telescope, Martin Pugh, Robert Gendler; 57(cr) Joseph Brimacombe/NASA; 58(c) John MacKenty (STScI) et al. & the Hubble Heritage Team (AURA/ STScI/ NASA); 59(b) NASA/JPL-Caltech, (bl) NASA, JPL-Caltech, WISE; 68–69(bg) NASA/CXC/M.Weiss; 69(cl) NASA/JPL-Caltech; 70(bl) NASA, ESA, Zolt Levay (StScI); 73(c) NASA, (br) NASA/JPL-Caltech; 74(c) X-ray: NASA/UMass/D.Wang et al., IR: NASA/STScI, (br) Alain Riazuelo; 75(c) NASA/Goddard Space Flight Center/Swift; 77(tl) Y. Izotov (Main Astronomical Obs., Ukraine), T. Thuan (Univ. Virginia), ESA, NASA; 77(b) NASA/CXC/JPL-Caltech/STScI, (bl) NASA/STScI/SAO, (bl) NASA/JPL-Caltech/GSFC, (bl) NASA/JPL-Caltech, (bl) NASA/JPL-Caltech, (bl) NASA/JPL-Caltech, (bl) NASA/JPL-Caltech/SAO/NOAO, (bl) NASA/CXC/JPL-Caltech/STScI/NSF/NRAO/VLA, (bl) NASA/JPL-Caltech/ESA/Harvard-Smithsonian CfA; 78–79(bg) Star Shadows Remote Observatory and PROMPT/CTIO (Steve Mazlin, Jack Harvey, Rick Gilbert, and Daniel Verschatse); 78(cl) Canada-France-Hawaii Telescope, J.-C. Cuillandre (CFHT), Coelum; 79(cr) Local Group Galaxies Survey Team, NOAO, AURA, NSF, (c) Hubble Heritage Team (STScI/AURA) Hubble Heritage (STScI/AURA) L. Jenkins (GSFC/U. Leicester); 83(tr) Northrop Grumman; 86(tr) NASA CXC/NGST, (br) X-ray: NASA/CXC/UMass/D.Wang et al., Optical: NASA/HST/D.Wang et al.; 87(cl) Ipac/Caltech/NASA, (c) NASA/JPL-Caltech/R. Hurt (SSC); 88(tr) NASA/Tim Pyle; 90(tr) NASA Ames/SETI Institute/JPL-Caltech; 91(bl) NASA; 94(bl) NASA-GRIN, (br) NASA Goddard Space Flight Center (NASA-GSFC); 95(tl) NASA Jet Propulsion Laboratory (NASA-JPL); 96–97 NASA-JPL; 98(cr) NASA-JPL; 99(clockwise from cl) NASA-JPL, NASA-GRIN, NASA-JPL, NASA-JPL; 108(bl) NASA-JPL; 110(cl) NASA-GRIN, (bc) NASA-JPL, (br) NASA-JPL; 115(br) NASA-JPL; 120–121(c) NASA-JPL; 121(tr) NASA Marshall Space Flight Center (NASA-MSFC), (bl) NASA-JPL; 125(tl) NASA-JPL, (c) NASA-MSFC; 128(br) NASA-JPL; 129(cr) NASA-JPL, (br) NASA-JPL; 137(b) JPL-Caltech; 141(bl); 142(c) JPL-Caltech, (t) NASA Langley Research Center (NASA-LaRC); 142–143(b); 146(bl); 146–147(t) Johns Hopkins University Applied Physics Laboratory/Southwest Research Institute; 148(c) JPL/University of Arizona; 148–149 oval insets JPL; 150(c); 151 Saturn JPL, Comet Borrelly JPL, Uranus, Neptune, Voyager 2 gold disk, Deep Space 1; 152(bl) STEREO; 153; 155(bl), (br); 158(bl) JPL/Cornell; 160–161(bg) JPL/Cornell; 160(bl) Goddard Space Flight Center Scientific Visualization Studio, Mariner 4 JPL, Mariner 9 JPL, Mars 3 Russian Space Research Institute (IKI), Viking lander, Mars Global Surveyor; 161 Sojourner JPL-Caltech, Spirit/Opportunity rover JPL, Mars Reconnaissance Orbiter JPL; 162–163(bg); 167(br); 169(c), (b); 172(bl) Johns Hopkins University Applied Physics Laboratory/Southwest Research Institute; 173(br); 174–175(bg) JPL-Caltech/T. Pyle (SSC); 176–177; 178(panel, b); 188(tr) NASA-GRIN; 194(m) NASA-GRIN; 198(bl) NASA-GRIN; 202(tl); 203(bl); 204–205(m) NASA-GRIN; 211(tl)

Paul & Kathryn Gray 71(bl) Max Starmus

Photolibrary.com 104–105 Steve Vidler

Photoshot 22(r)

Reuters 137(t) Kimimasa Mayama

Rex Features 47(cr) REX/Everett Collection; 113(cr) Nils Jorgensen; 155(tl); 163(br) NASA; 174(tl) Everett Collection, (c) c.Paramount/Everett; 175(b) KeystoneUSA-ZUMA; 190(tl) Everett Collection, (tr); 200(b); 201(cl) Snap Stills; 215(br) c.20thC.Fox/Everett; 216–217(m) Paramount Pictures/courtesy Everett Collection; 217(br) c.Universal/Everett